HÉLOÏSE IS BALD

Émilie de Turckheim

Héloïse is Bald

Translated from the French by Sophie Lewis

JONATHAN CAPE
LONDON

1 3 5 7 9 10 8 6 4 2

Jonathan Cape, an imprint of Vintage,
20 Vauxhall Bridge Road,
London SW1V 2SA

Jonathan Cape is part of the Penguin Random House group of companies whose addresses can be
found at global.penguinrandomhouse.com.

First published by Jonathan Cape in 2015

www.vintage-books.co.uk

A CIP catalogue record for this book is available from the British Library

ISBN 9780224097857

Printed and bound in Great Britain
by Clays Ltd, St Ives plc

Typeset in Cartier Book Pro 11.5/15 pt by
Palimpsest Book Production Limited, Falkirk, Stirlingshire

This book is supported by the Institut français (Royaume-Uni) as part of the Burgess programme.

Penguin Random House is committed to a sustainable future for our business, our readers and our
planet. This book is made from Forest Stewardship Council® certified paper.

For Krishna

DONNA ELVIRA

Non ti fidar, o misera,
Di quel ribaldo cor!
Me già tradì quel barbaro,
Te vuol tradir ancor.

Don Giovanni, scena 12, atto I
(Lorenzo da Ponte)

DONNA ELVIRA

Do not believe, unhappy one,
In that faithless heart!
The villain has already betrayed me!
Now he seeks to betray you.

Don Giovanni, scene 12 act I
(Lorenzo da Ponte)
[Translation by William Murray]

I

Héloïse is bald. She still has a long life ahead of her. Her dress has the anxious stiffness of new clothes. Not a single smudge of varnish spoils her short red nails. Upright in her high chair, she is lower than the others, her toes squeezed into a pair of ballet slippers that struggle to contain the plump flesh of her feet. Mirabelle has stretched a shawl between the armrests so that Héloïse will not slip down. The shawl smells of Mirabelle's skin: seaweed, the sea urchin's orange flesh, the green-black depths of the Mediterranean. Nobody is paying attention to Héloïse. Sometimes a face looms near, eyes, blue ones, hazel, glasses, someone strokes her cheek, her poor pink head. Héloïse does not speak. She snatches the biscuit that a child holds out to her, stuffs it into her mouth and chomps. Mirabelle pushes her index finger between Héloïse's lips and fishes out the revolting, colourless, chewed-up petit four. Héloïse does not protest. She is used to people taking food out of her mouth. It's for her own good. She nods sweetly. She is hardly there. She has no idea of the names, ages or lives of these people, nor of the children concealed within the room's heavy furnishings, or the lace hems edging the little girls' ankles, nor of her grumpy father sat by himself in a corner, turning the pages of a catalogue of African art, *The*

Splendour of the Dogon, nor of the fir tree weighed down with angels and Christmas baubles that reflect the guests' shifting faces in the shape of biscuits, potatoes or wine glasses. Héloïse's gaze skips to Justine's hat and veil, to the bottle of nail polish in Justine's hand, the red tablecloth, the Father Christmas gingerbread men, the mini toast with lumpfish caviar, the blinis, the baby tomatoes each topped with a caper and skewered by a toothpick, the clammy gleam of the smoked salmon, the crème fraîche, its plastic tub exchanged for a Chinese ramekin, and Violette, the translucent blonde woman, sunk deep in a chaise longue, an infant in the crook of her arm. Violette would like to throw the baby into the fire.

He was born during the snowstorm, at midnight, a week ago; Violette called the man she loves. 'Lawrence, come and fetch me, it's coming – now! He's being born, he's coming out! I can see the top of his head! He has red hair! He's Irish!' The man asked her to calm herself: 'Calm down,' he said, three times. He said she was thoughtless, calling him at home, she could have woken his wife. Then, more gently, he said that he had gone into the passage to pick up the other telephone, that Violette must be reasonable, sensible, that she was putting him in an extremely delicate situation. The threatening way he pronounced the word 'extremely'. He couldn't come, no, he didn't have to, he was sorry, he would order a taxi to pick her up from right outside her door – better, an ambulance, and he would think of her every step of the way. For Violette, a thought, even a long one, was not good enough, because he used to hover around her like a stubborn, noisy black dung fly. First a present, the photo of the Melanesian women that he had sent to the riding centre where Violette worked, then the letters, romantic ones, the flowers, red ones, the Michelin-starred restaurants, the dusky wine that a young sommelier with a crew cut had poured into the flared decanter like a precious chemical poison, the white lights of a film theatre on his stubbly throat, the sofas on which she was kissed into submission, the breasts squeezed in a stinking horsebox at the riding centre, the delicious saliva, the teeth, the taste of tobacco, the concert hall and the tense gallop of a Perspex piano that displayed its hammers and wiry innards for all to see, a Mozart opera and his fingers, each in turn inside her, even the fourth finger with the ring that bound him to the other woman, the thumb brutally deep in her vagina as Donna Elvira sang '*Non ti fidar!*' and Don Giovanni's foul mouth, the schemes tossed like baby worms into the gaping wide gullet of a down-and-out fledgling, the journeys, the oceans crossed, the cetaceans ridden, the Mariana Trench traversed, the sales room at Hageru Auction House in Tokyo and the blood vessels pumped when they won the lot – a fifteenth-century Muromachi painting showing three catfish hanging from the branches of a free-floating cherry tree – the hotels with their spotless white dressing gowns, their ward-robes full of space and mahogany shoehorns, disposable slippers, embroidered kimonos, ranks of expensive skin creams, stacks of notepaper with the hotel's initials watermarked in silver-edged relief, the pink palace overlooking the Ganges, the Gritti Palace on the Grand Canal, the suites with lobby, lounge, boudoir, smoking room and windows looking out over the Herengracht canal, Times Square or the Île Saint-Louis, the tiny, feather-light lace slips wrapped in tissue paper, and the jewel-lery, she who did not wear jewellery.

'I don't fucking care if I wake your wife! I'm not giving

birth without you! You can send me a fire engine, a Red Cross plane – I shan't set foot in any of them! You have to come and get me right now – Lawrence! My waters have broken! He's coming already!' The man wanted to raise his voice but he couldn't do that, he whispered, it was pitch-dark in the passage where he was crouching, with the smell of beeswax, family, domestic order, the sweet breathing of his two daughters sleeping behind their bedroom doors. He told Violette that she must stop talking nonsense, the child's head was not coming out right now, she must calm down and think of the baby. 'No, it's you, you spineless shit, you're the one who should be thinking of the baby!' He did not get angry. He said that they had had an affair – inside, the baby pummelled her sides with its feet – and even more gently and carefully spelled out, as you speak to a sick person, to an old lady, a madwoman, that he was not the father of the child she was expecting and that he had no reason to accompany her to the hospital. And Violette thought: *You piece of shit, there are hundreds of reasons, you promised me this and that and the other, nobody gives birth alone, except giraffes and sows, you promised me so many things, I'm shaking and I've finished the bottle of pills that calm me down, let me sleep, knock me out like they knock out tuna on ships' bridges with a bludgeon. I should have had an abortion, what a word, soon as it's born I'll give it away, I won't even look at its tiny man's face.* Violette hadn't wanted to end up threatening him and now she was making threats. Stealthily, taking care that his steps did not squeak on the parquet, on that amber-waxed surface, Lawrence dressed. In the entrance hall he picked up the car keys from the lacquered console with its thoroughbred lines, bought with Violette, last autumn after a stroll in Central Park beneath the scarlet and gold leaves. He had been taking part in a conference and she had joined him there, in New York. They had served Violette champagne on the plane. Thoroughly drunk, she had told the stewardess that she was the happiest woman in the world. Lawrence drove fast; he did not knock on Violette's door; she had done her make-up for him. He came in and cut through the living room like a man in his own home. Violette had slipped on a slinky dress with fish scale sequins. The lift was broken. He gathered Violette into his arms and rebuked her for her ridiculous, inappropriate clothing. She cried tears of joy. He was there, in his woollen peacoat, really there, sweating from having hurried, elegant in spite of himself, as at every other moment in his life. She embraced him, thanked him. She gave him no choice; he came out of pity – and so that she wouldn't go and say anything stupid. She said: 'Shush, be quiet, I love your beautiful eyes when you get all worked up.' All the way down the stairs, her bracelets and necklaces made a rattling sound. Inside the car, the scales of the fish dress shimmered, gleaming golds, the street lights scattered away, the night shot through with gilded car beams, oblique snowflakes. The hospital appeared deserted in the snow. The midwife's name was Emilie, it was written on her pastel-pink scrubs, and she put a finger deep into Violette's vagina. Emilie said that she was very advanced, nine centimetres dilated, goodness, Violette should have come to the hospital sooner instead of dolling herself up, decking herself with jewellery, in this dress, like a tart left out in the cold! Where did she think she was? This was a maternity ward – not a catwalk! But never mind, now Violette had to gather all her strength, breathe through her nose, she was going to have a baby as cute as any and the midwife's smiling voice was a model of tenderness and admonishment. Violette asked the man to swear he would do everything that he should do, that he would go with them, the baby and her, to the zoo every second Sunday, to stroke the sheep in Suffolk and the giant rabbits in Flanders. 'Tell me you won't be one of those pathetic married bastards who fuck a girl for months and then scuttle away like cockroaches the morning after the birth,' she pants. The man said she was as crazy as ever. Emilie got angry. They needed to concentrate on her breathing and the contractions. She had to push. Violette pushed. The baby was tearing her anus apart. Astonishing how much this hurt. A rifle-butt beating at her lower back. Her mother had lied. She had promised that it was like the cramps you get with diarrhoea. The man said he preferred to wait in the corridor. Emilie was very young. She gave an order. She delivered ten children a day: she was a powerful woman. People obeyed her instinctively. She put the man's hand into Violette's. The man felt her nails, wild with emotion, with pathetic hope, digging into his skin. Suddenly Violette was happy. 'We're going to have a baby!' Lawrence snatched his fingers away from the sweating, loving hand. Violette fainted. The baby was born by Caesarian. Violette said she didn't want it. 'How on earth?' exclaimed the midwife, the doctor and the nurse. 'He is the most beautiful present life can give!' They laid the baby down beside Violette. Violette turned her back to him. On the third day, she gave him a name.

The fire is making her cheeks burn; someone must have put another log on. Violette looks down at her baby, Barnabé. He is wearing a jumpsuit, booties with pompoms, a red woollen jacket with large, wobbly stitches, knitted hell-for-leather in four days by Mirabelle, Violette's older sister. Violette hears a voice. Deep, sure of itself, tempered by a hint of Irish. It is Lawrence. Then a laugh, distinct, rectilinear, paralysing as a poison arrow. It is Lawrence's wife, Fleur. Idiotic name. Nicknamed Tilala by Lawrence since the start of their relationship. Idiotic nickname. Dr Lawrence Calvagh, head consultant of the Emergencies division at Robert-Koch Paediatric Hospital, and Fleur, star ballerina, now retired. Violette allows her eyes to follow Fleur, who takes her daughter by the arm. The pine tree's sap oozes the length of the branches.

'Justine! You've got polish all over Héloïse's nails!'

'She didn't blubber an' I done it nicely.'

'Speak properly! I've had enough of this obsession. You're annoying everyone!'

'Everyone said I could.'

Applying the red varnish to obedient nails – intoxicating! Justine likes St Nicholas's Day. An infinity of docile nails. She starts with the children's nails, giving them no choice in the matter. She asks permission from the adults. The women are already wearing nail varnish: they excuse themselves, show their hands, say no. But the men say yes. They don't want to be killjoys. Justine reassures them, she is persuasive, a drop of remover will be enough to take it all off, it won't leave a trace, it will be as if nothing had happened. They give a *hmmm* of uncertainty while abandoning their nails to her attentions. They continue their conversation, hold their half-smoked cigarettes or half-empty glasses in their other hands, and forget Justine who, on her knees, predatory and perfectionist, is deflowering their nails. There is art in her movements; there is soul, sensuality; she does not varnish nails by chance or out of boredom, she varnishes nails with a theatrical singularity of vision and great waves of joy. The men always say yes. Justine is eleven years old and looks thirteen in her dress and her hat with its veil, all retrieved from deep within a leather suitcase in Jeanne's room; salvaged out of that sculpture of compressed material, a condensed mass of skirts and blouses, memories of winters and summers, of disappointments, hopes and resentments laid down in fabric.

Héloïse does not speak. The world around her has no meaning beyond the soft, blurry voices, their music woven together, a sneeze, a burst of laughter, a fit of coughing; no shape beyond the curving oval of the chaise longue where Violette is cradling Barnabé, no greater attraction than the glittering baubles in the branches of the tree. Héloïse's skin has no wrinkles, no history. Long black lashes guard her shark-like, all-seeing eyes. Héloïse is a thousand years old. The eternal face of humanity rewound to the very beginning. Héloïse is five months old. She is a stunning baby, born early, in July, at the scorching siesta hour, at the hospital in Ajaccio, so suddenly that the doctor had to hold the head already emerging from Mirabelle's vagina in his smooth, gloved left hand, while the midwife rolled the other latex glove onto his right. With a feeling that was not sorrow – the breakdown, the ice, the effects of a curse? – Mirabelle had always thought that she would not have a child, because of the spill and the blood of an abortion in Switzerland, in a scratchy nightdress, which must have spoiled everything. She fell pregnant at forty. 'At your age I'd already been a mother for twenty years, not to mention that at that age the skin on your belly never really recovers and the chances are you'll be giving us a Down's baby,' (her mother, Jeanne). Mirabelle unties the shawl, seizes Héloïse under her arms and swings her up – she is light, a kitten, only seven kilos – sits her on the chaise longue, her lolling head propped up by a cushion. Her minuscule varnished fingernails match the knitted jacket Barnabé is wearing as he feeds at Violette's breast. There is a fissure, a hairline crack, on the areola. Every time the child sucks it's like hot chilli on this wound. Mirabelle kneels and observes the two babies, Héloïse and Barnabé, through the camera's viewfinder. 'Baptiste, could you take Héloïse's dummy out, please?' Baptiste goes on reading and his hand mimes an empty punch. ('I come to your mother's house with you every year for this godawful St Nicholas tea, don't ask any more of me.') Mirabelle blushes. 'Lawrence, please, could you take Héloïse's dummy out?' Lawrence is used to infants. He handles them. He saves their lives. He tugs on the plastic ring and Héloïse feels the dummy slip away. Distortion of her little arched brows and the tremulous chin goes down. Mirabelle is annoyed. 'My Héloïse! Smile nicely! My little bunny! Smile nicely for the camera!' The scene looks nothing like the photo of which she dreams: Héloïse, pink and delicious in her new dress, new ballet slippers, smile full of love, silken sofa, baby Barnabé at Violette's milk-swollen breast, fire in the hearth, gold-decked Christmas tree, familial contentment. Screams. 'Sweetness! Just one pretty smile!' The scream fluctuates. The ebb and flow of a bawling temptress. Héloïse is red-faced, turning blue-black, gasping. The family, friends, everything stops: talk, games, mastication. All turn to the enraged black hole of a mouth. 'I believe your daughter has a problem.' Héloïse's cries drown

Mirabelle's voice. Baptiste points at Mirabelle, at her stomach. She must have made a mistake. She feels her cheeks flush hotly. Héloïse's bicoloured dribble is staining the chaise longue's beige- and wine-coloured stripes. Lawrence restores the dummy to the unhinged little gob. Héloïse spits it out again. The dummy rolls up to Baptiste's feet, wetting one sole. Advice is given. 'She should be distracted with a rattle or a lighter flame.' 'Force the dummy into her mouth.' 'Go for a walk with her in the pram.' 'Bathe her in a valerian root infusion.' 'Sing her a lullaby; you were almost a singer, Lawrence, you could do it, you could sing her something calming.' (Someone says, 'Perhaps she just didn't want her photo taken.') Heads crane towards the regal, demonic little body. Never has anyone seen such a fit of fury. A life in howls. Baptiste's eyes bore into Mirabelle. He is handsome, a cellist, a man of few words, deep as a cold well. Baptiste cannot be everything at once, Mirabelle reasons. *He is not the perfect father to Héloïse, but I have my faults too, I lose things, I go into a room and forget what I came for, I don't understand classical music, I like love songs, show music, I listen to crap, Baptiste says. I'm never really turned on. There are people who can always get turned on. In restaurants I don't know how to choose between one dish and another. I tell Baptiste: choose for me. If they'd all stop watching me, I could take Héloïse in my arms, rock her and kiss her cheeks, and if that doesn't work I'll give her a slap, and if that doesn't work, I'll give her a good shaking 'til she stops bawling. My wee tiny baby. My darling. All the moves and all the words that all mothers know. Where are they?*

Mirabelle asks Lawrence to do something, as if the situation were anything to do with medicine. *A pill, an injection, a Chinese massage*, Mirabelle thinks. Lawrence kneels. He would like to know where Héloïse finds the spirit to scream without restraint, without compromise. In her screams there is love, desperation, astonishment at being alive. Lawrence would like to have the strength and the immodesty to be alive the way that Héloïse is furious. He dreams of an existence in which every gesture and every word would be equally extreme. It would mean beating time at its own headlong race. Lawrence strokes Héloïse's face, the spit at the corners of her mouth, and, feeling his thumb moving over her lips, Héloïse sucks at it. And, screams over, she sucks, passionately. She sucks as one swallows a river after tearing through a summer, slopes of poppies at full tilt, white dresses, bare feet, burning plains. In the living room, everyone can hear the fire crackling and the thumb being devoured, hints of kisses. Being sucked, Lawrence trembles. Héloïse falls in love.

II

II

Héloïse loves the smell of seriousness and disinfectant in the blue lino-tiled corridors, the long, bleak facade of sullen concrete, the spiny shrubs in the car park borders, the strip-lights' glow in the low panelled ceilings, queasy, distorting the skin, the ambulance drivers smoking and sharing a slice of Madeira cake between them, hunched against the cold. Héloïse would have sacrificed all her toys in exchange for permission to travel in the Robert-Koch Paediatric Hospital's ambulance just once a week. The snow has already covered the markings in the car park and is now making inroads with the bins, the parked cars and the three benches, which are deserted but for a magpie frozen to his perch on one of them, waiting for the end of the cigarette break and the resulting cake crumbs. Héloïse runs her mitten over the snow-covered body of a Renault 5, then of a Peugeot 104. A trickle of icy water runs down her wrist. Think of paper torn to pieces, footprints in deep snow. The glass doors slide magically away before her just as her impatient little boots step onto the ridged anti-slip matting. Mirabelle lies spreadeagled on the ice. She waves to the ambulance drivers not to move. 'Nothing's broken!' Her voice is snatched away by the white spirals of a rare Parisian blizzard.

Jubilant waiting room: wounds flecked with gravel, arms

wrapped in scarves, graveyard faces, the soft tears of infants drunk with fever, congealed red compresses, black eyes. A feast for the senses. A young rider in high boots lying on a stretcher pushes away his mother's hand as she scolds him and strokes his hair: 'That's what did it, you silly thing! It's your helmet that saved you!' A greenish baby has just vomited on the box of building bricks and incomplete puzzles set out for the children. A little girl in a Zorro costume plunges her rapier between her clenched thighs. You'd think she had nothing at all wrong with her. Héloïse's favourite character is a roving, red-headed and wrinkled witch, cuckoo-clock tucked under her arm, dressed in a tattered wedding gown and a little goose down jacket, pilfered the previous winter from a loud-mouthed patient who had come to Emergencies with a story about a dart and a punctured eye. The bride knows the names of all the nurses. They give her paracetamol, glasses of water, tissues, waterproof boots, survival blankets silvered on one side and gold on the other. On New Year's Eve, the bride is allowed a slice of Christmas cake and a glass of fizz. She spends her evenings in the well-heated waiting room. She shrieks at the top of her voice: 'And those sons of bitches just loved seeing me bald as a baby!'

Héloïse is four years old and has thirteen stitches. On the left side: her thumb and elbow; on the right: in her eyebrow and her chin. Tonight, at midnight, in her scalp. Lawrence says that scars are the skin's trophies, the indelible tattoos of temerity. Héloïse waits. Not the nurse; not the house doctor; the king. Absorbed by her ponderings about the king, who devotes himself to the saddest and most complicated emergencies – cases of meningitis, internal haemorrhages, bad tibial fractures, acute peritonitis, bleach poisonings, electrocutions, infants dehydrated by diarrhoea, crumpled as prunes. The king will make an exception for Héloïse. He will look after her minor nick and he'll say that he has never seen such a *stoical* little girl. Surely a compliment. A token of love. He says it every time.

Héloïse can't bear to wait for her king any longer. She stands up and runs as fast as she can between the rows of orange chairs, plucked from a metro platform. Mirabelle waves for her to sit down. She's almost inclined to whistle, as if calling a dog. Héloïse knocks into a pram which rolls forward on the lino, hits the wall and begins to cry. 'You have woken a baby! Well done, Héloïse!' Mirabelle apologises to the mother (*Too young*, thinks Mirabelle. *How can you care for a child when you're still a child yourself, with childish eyes, still wanting to be comforted?*) who bends sullenly over the pram and strokes her baby's dry, feverish forehead. Héloïse has never been one to walk. Everything about her rushes and bolts: her confident words, sudden notions, her cousin Barnabé whom she drags every Saturday to the foot of the Deadly Dipper, out of bounds to all under-sevens, which gives Barnabé nightmares and attracts Héloïse like a magnet.

Héloïse speeds up, racing past dehydrated babies, stretchers, the reception desk where the old red-head in her wedding dress is lounging, pointing a finger at two bored nurses, hollering that sooner or later she will lay her hands on the bastards who stopped her from marrying Hans-Jakob.

'Your Héloïse is quite a little whirlwind!'

Always that hint of an Irish accent, behind the slightly

suppressed, muffled 'r's, gentler than the French 'r'. Lawrence left Dublin at the age of twelve but his lips have retained a pinch of Irishness that sweetens and spices his words. He kisses Mirabelle on one cheek.

'So what happened, little lion.'

Héloïse points at the top of her head.

'She climbed Violette's bookshelves like a Fury . . . We were having dinner at Violette's – and the whole bookcase fell over on top of her.'

'I see.'

'All just to reach a photograph.'

'A nice photo of the family . . . ?'

'No, it was that photo of the black women; you know . . .'

(Lawrence does not know, or pretends he doesn't.)

'You do; you gave it to Violette . . . Those black women held in the Botanical Gardens.'

Lawrence's feelings are entirely under control. Nothing troubles his smile.

'Follow me, Héloïse. We shall have to cut off this pretty head of yours. It's the only solution.'

Lawrence is going to cut her head off with a saw. He will tell her she is stoical. Héloïse's heart is thumping. In her enchanted tummy, a small frantic animal, a hamster, is trotting inside a wheel as fast as it can.

'Am I going to die?'

'Hmm . . . There's a strong chance that you will.'

'But if I'm deaded, can I still go to bed with you?'

Mirabelle claps her hand over Héloïse's mouth. Wishes she'd done it less violently.

'What did you say? She meant to say sleep . . . just . . . to

16

take a nap . . . but not . . . She doesn't even know what that means!'

Lawrence takes Héloïse's chin between finger and thumb.

'Do you really want to sleep with me? Don't you think I'm a bit old?'

'How old're you?'

'Wait a minute while I count . . . I believe I'm forty-four years old.'

'Is that more or less than a thousand?'

'Less. But I am . . . just a second . . . eleven times older than you.'

'Eleven times! I've never seen anyone so old!'

'Don't say that, little lion . . .'

'Are you going to die soon?'

'No, I have a few springs left in me yet.'

'And no winters?'

'Yes, some winters too . . . I still have plenty of seasons ahead of me.'

Héloïse, Mirabelle and Lawrence are walking down a hallway disfigured by long black lines traced, over the years, by stretchers scraping against the walls. Lawrence walks quickly, ahead of the mother and daughter, through the maze of blue corridors. He met Mirabelle at high school and he knows the story of her life: her childhood in Algeria, the fig trees' sickening scent in the garden of paradise, the greenhouse where her father's alien creatures used to grow, feathered cacti and red-sapped carnivorous plants, Assim's tongue, dumbstruck at the summit of Aïdour, in the delighted mouth of breathless, twelve-year-old Mirabelle, leaning over the ramparts of the

17

Santa Cruz fort above Oran, their calves pricked by the tragic agaves which only flower once before dying and so which, basically, 'die of having flowered' – in Mirabelle's mother Jeanne's words, who used to call her husband 'Dodo', seeing in him a resemblance to the great, clumsy, vanished bird of Mauritius, and who was listening to *'C'était une cannibale'* – 'There was once a cannibal lady' – when Dodo, whose given name was Georges, locked himself inside the magic greenhouse with Mirabelle's nanny to make her cry out in Arabic among the gold and red limbs of the extraordinary plants. Lawrence knows of the rain that was falling on the port of Oran the morning Mirabelle and her mother, landed with a belly full to bursting, held their Algerian life at arm's length, reduced to four leather suitcases, waiting for the ocean liner on the bridge of which Violette would be born and Mirabelle would vomit the sweet pastries guzzled on the sly, fig-stuffed and plain almond *tcharek*, after hearing the first, tiny and astonishing cry from her sister, smeared with stickiness and blood. Lawrence can still hear the giant hailstones, deafening on the roof of the barn where all the schoolchildren had taken refuge, except for the strange new girl, born in Oran and named for a small yellow plum, hands and face straining up into the hostile sky, white with shooting stones. He remembers the hurrying hours, secrets on the bench in the Church of St Paul, his knee held away from Mirabelle's by an empty space as impenetrable as wood; and the Alsatian woman praying in traditional costume, kneeling right there, keeping an angry eye on the irresolute lovers. One morning, her hair invisible beneath a great black bow, she had stopped at the confessional in order to catch, through the filigreed wooden panel, the two profiles in the act of sacrilegious embrace. Thirty years had flown by and Lawrence has not forgotten the jutting collarbone, the bony back he had embraced, noting each bump in the spine, the liquid vagina licked out in student digs on the rue des Saints-Pères, the conversation in the carnelian-red 2CV parked outside the building, under a blazing, leaden sun, unable to ease pregnant Mirabelle's isolation, and Lawrence's alarm as he heard Mirabelle's disjointed words unfold one by one inside that stifling cell, like poisoned blossoms. Hands on the wheel, silently he recited his father Laoghaire's words to himself: *Life is too short for mistakes. Don't make them.*

Héloïse is the heroine of that precious night. It is the witching hour, midnight, when Lawrence's stirring, long-lashed eyes focus on the razor cutting through the hair with its glints of chestnut, whisky, full moons and buttered corn, in drifts on the lino, little by little covering the baby-blue hospital slippers. On the scalp, the wound is shaped like a mouth holding back a smile. Héloïse sees the curls fall, fall, fall. And it's as if her temperature, her joy, are falling along with them. As if her temperature and her joy are mingling at Lawrence's feet, with the poor hair, the hospital odour of sacrifice and disinfectant. Héloïse feels lonely: abandoned by her hair, by her mother who is looking out of the window, far into the night, at the snowed-in cars in the car park, abandoned by Lawrence's hand which, in four stitches' time, will leave her behind and return to its heroic round of bodies to repair.

The needle has pierced her scalp and Héloïse did not flinch even a little. Lawrence forgets to tell her that she has been stoical. Héloïse feels a tear boiling up, clinging to her eye, and only just manages to hold it back with all the strength of her pride, sucks it back in as, in the far reaches of childhood, she used to suck Lawrence's thumb. 'I've had to cut off a fair bit of hair but it'll grow back in two shakes of a lamb's tail. Look at that, my little lion! Angel hair! The sun's own mane!' Lawrence has picked up a lock from the blue floor and slips it into his shirt pocket. Héloïse feels a delicious stab; believes she must be happy for the rest of her days. She covers her mouth with her hand for fear of letting her joy show and of being scolded for having climbed the bookcase, infuriated her father, incited her father's hands to close around Mirabelle's shaken neck, forced Mirabelle to drive her through the snow. Lawrence approaches Mirabelle, whose weary head comes to rest on his high-up shoulder. He hugs Mirabelle and Mirabelle responds with a tighter embrace, which might be the embrace of former lovers, the solid embrace of friendship or the embrace of one contrary spark that has outlasted the decades, and that burns and hurts, and nourishes a horribly sad, stupid, heartbreaking hope.

Héloïse points to Lawrence's heart, pressed against her mother's heart. (*Lawrence, I don't love you.*) The adults look at her.

III

Violette's wrist disappears into a plaster cast decorated with unicorns, rainbows, hearts, scribbles, bandy-legged ponies, get better soon messages, painstaking and wobbly names. Violette looks at the slightly blurred photo, given to her by Lawrence eight years earlier: two Melanesian women in an enclosure in the Botanical Gardens, black breasts, black eyes watching her through the paper. On the back of the photo the ink is faded from too many readings. Lawrence's urgent handwriting.

> *Dear Violette,*
> *This is not a silly bit of trivia, as you so ignorantly declared on*
> *Saturday, but shows the 111 Melanesians who were exhibited*
> *like monkeys in the Botanical Gardens in the Bois de Boulogne.*
> *Parisians threw peanuts to them. Dine with me.*
> *L*

Images of their year, which was really just seven months, the birth, life and death of their love, parade through Violette's mind in the accelerated style of a silent film, with two faces radiant in the light of the projectors, miming emotions to excess: astonishment, lightheartedness, delight, the misery of the words 'The End'. They had met on the bridge called Pont au Double – just the right name, Violette often thought, for a man both endlessly big and vanishingly small, golden and sod, the model two-faced lover in fact – which crosses the Seine and leads to the public square in front of Notre Dame. Above the untroubled water, Lawrence had taken her by the wrist and kissed her. Three days earlier, he had sent the photo, rolled up and tied with a ribbon, to the riding centre where Violette taught her young riders the art of holding their reins like an open book. She had sat down on a bench beneath the bits and bridles. The Melanesian women seemed to invite her to join them on the other side of the wire, in the imitation house that hadn't even been made for them – in 1929 the Ethnographic Exhibition's Senegalese people had slept beneath the same false roof.

Their love story had begun a few days before she received the photo, at Lawrence's home, the apartment on rue de Rivoli, at a 'buffet supper' such as Fleur loved to organise and which would end with dancing, the world put to rights, men drunkenly playing the piano, and then daybreak, the slate-grey dawn, scalding cups of coffee on the long balcony above the plunging drop to the Tuileries gardens. Sat on top of the billiard table – which suffered a regular battering on these buffet supper nights: the number of wine glass circles and cigarette burns in the green baize was now countless – Lawrence was relating how his newly married father Laoghaire and mother Margareth had gone to the 1931 Colonial Exhibition in Paris, the one put on by Marshal Lyautey. One woman, a cousin of Fleur, had said that the Marshal was – and she had it from a reliable source – homosexual. And then a man, Pierre Klein, an anaesthetist at the Robert-Koch Paediatric Hospital, had reported what Georges Clémenceau had said of the Marshal: 'He is an admirable, courageous man who has always had balls of steel . . . even if they weren't always his own balls.' There were fits of cackling and the billiard table fielded a dousing of champagne. One woman said: 'I already knew that one.' As no one heard her, she gave Violette's sleeve a tug and whispered into her ear: 'I already knew it, Clémenceau's joke.' A childhood friend of Lawrence and literature professor at the Sorbonne said that Marshal Lyautey had been Proust's model for the character of the Baron de Charlus. A number of heads nodded.

'Really?' (The anaesthetist.)

'That's interesting.' (Fleur's cousin.)

'I had no idea.' (Another woman.)

'You don't even know who Proust is.' (Her husband, for the benefit of the company.)

Violette looked at Lawrence who was already looking at her. She smiled at him, raised her glass and, ignoring the others, who were busy giggling and discussing the Baron de Charlus, they toasted each other. The anaesthetist asked: 'Who here has actually read *À la recherche du temps perdu?*' Everyone lied in turn. Lawrence started talking again. Everyone stopped talking so as to listen, except for Violette who was having fun contradicting him and parrotting childishly after him, in a monotone, every sentence as he spoke it: 'A hundred and eleven Melanesians who were dumped in the Botanical Garden and made to dance, shaking their cartoon-comic savage faces, to give wild animal cries, to eat raw meat before the very eyes of the people of Paris, of all the over-fed rubbernecks with their pot-bellies.' Violette sniggered, saying that it was all made up, letting her dress strap slip off her shoulder and pulling it up again, wishing Lawrence would push her down on the billiard table and cover her with kisses. 'Of course they had fun! It was the high point of their lives . . . Paris, all expenses paid . . . fed, housed, laundry done . . . The most beautiful city in the world! Really, it was pearls before swine!' They could see all her pretty teeth when she burst out laughing. Lawrence spoke of the Melanesians who, having only just arrived in Paris, were shipped to the zoo in Frankfurt in exchange for the crocodiles – which travelled to Paris in order to replace their cold-blooded cousins whom poor nutrition had killed a few days before the opening of the Exhibition. Violette laughed even harder, called Lawrence a buttress against the injustices of this cruel world and looked around among the other guests for abetment in her spite, but nobody volunteered. Lawrence pointed at her – he was, at last, furious. Violette felt that simple childhood joy when, after very many throws of the dice, she won at snakes and ladders.

Violette digs a finger under her plaster cast to scratch but the itch is further in. She has only to close her eyes to hear that beautiful, deep, furiously musical voice in the great salon at rue de Rivoli where the whimsical Fleur fluttered from one guest to the next, distributing champagne, canapés of skewered summer fruit and Cuban cigars.

The thunderous voice of Héloïse in the corridor, the hurried patter of her cousin Barnabé, and Mirabelle, annoyed: 'Less noise, please! She might be asleep!' Violette hides the Melanesian women between two volumes of the Larousse encyclopaedia. Héloïse comes in without knocking, followed by Barnabé, and they both make a beeline for the plaster cast, turn it around in every direction to inspect the new drawings and read the words of encouragement. Mirabelle glances round the bedroom: drawn curtains, box of chocolates untouched on the desk, electric lighting in spite of the bright spring day outside, the sharp smell of a plate of congealed, grey chicken wings. Mirabelle prepares to say that the place could do with some air, changes her mind, gives the bouquet to her sister. Seventy poppies.

'Here, Violette, sweetheart . . . They'll have wilted in an hour . . .'

Poppies are Violette's favourite flower. Touchingly fragile, they live, flaming and red, and die.

'Did they behave themselves?'

'They cut Poseidon in two and put him back in the fishbowl.'

'Shit.'

Barnabé says he was already dead; he was floating on his side. Héloïse says he was just a goldfish. They have found some felt tips to colour in the cast: Barnabé slowly, in no hurry, his face pale and inexpressive, not allowing himself to go over the edges of legs and flanks; Héloïse in a rush, disfiguring a galloping pony, giving him a lion's mane, pink hooves and a jet engine-powered saddle.

'Be gentle with Violette's arm, you kids!'

'Oh, let them . . .'

Beside her sister, Mirabelle feels as if she is holding back words that threaten to flood from her pursed lips.

'Did your students come to see you? Your cast is covered in drawings . . .'

'All twelve of them! Even Anaïs . . . the little one who's a bit . . . I met her parents; they told me it's a condition similar to autism . . . but it's not exactly . . . it's not as serious . . . People scare her but she has a gift with horses . . . She goes right up close to them and looks them in the eye . . .'

'Violette, are you going to spend the whole time going on about an eight-year-old girl I've never set eyes on?'

A cold, mean shiver runs down the back of Mirabelle's neck. The acute note of spite, in her own throat. She swallows. The box of chocolates has not been opened. The best *chocolatier* in the neighbourhood. An exorbitant price. A violet ribbon, specially chosen for Violette. Four layers separated by slips of gold card. Complex chocolates, delicious just to look at. Mirabelle would like to say: 'You've not touched my chocolates.' She will have to say it in a playful or gently concerned tone. Mirabelle senses that she will not achieve the right tone of voice.

'Have you had time to try my chocolates?'

'No. Help yourself if you want some.'

'I chose the ribbon myself . . . well, the colour of it.'

'Red?'

'No, it's violet. It's your colour.'

'Do you remember Félicien, your boyfriend from school, who used to have lunch with us at home? And *maman* always saying: "I made sure to buy Saint-Félicien at the *fromagerie*."'

'Why do you mention that?'

'Do you think I look tired?'

'You have black circles under your eyes. Aren't you sleeping any better?'

'No. I could do with some needles . . . You wouldn't happen to have any knitting needles?'

'You know I knit . . .'

'I want to get them under the cast so I can scratch . . . It's driving me crazy not being able to scratch myself! It itches so much that it stops me sleeping . . . I turn the light back on and I spend the night trying to understand why Cronos . . .'

'Stop . . .'

'No! He went mad! As soon as I went inside his box, I felt it . . . He looked like he was seeing things . . . I don't understand why he hurt me!'

'He's a horse.'

'Mira, when you mount a horse, you feel that horse's heat in your thighs . . . He feels your heat in his skin . . . He gallops and you enter right into his gallop . . . You feel the hooves thundering in your belly and it's the horse that decides to keep you on his back because if he feels like it . . . at any time he can throw you to the ground and crush you flat, smash all your bones; he weighs 450 kilos. You can't imagine the strength a horse has and the love that he communicates . . . We are two animals, one on top of the other . . .'

Mirabelle thinks that they should rein their conversation back onto safer ground, but all her ideas have their down sides.

'Are you in love with your horse?'

'You sell sponges and washing-up liquid. You work in order to earn money, not to feel your body explode with love.'

Violette, her little baby sister, who bugs her, who has always bugged her. Twelve years ahead and so many scars.

'How's Barnabé? Is he getting on better at school?'

'He reads really well when he's at home . . . He can read a whole page aloud, without stumbling at all . . . But in class he still has this stammer . . .'

Barnabé giggles and buries his head in Violette's lap.

'Has he been asking questions again?'

Violette puts a finger to her lips. Shh.

'You can finish colouring me in later! Go and eat your tea . . . There is bread and apricot jam . . .'

Héloïse has already dragged Barnabé out into the corridor.

'And biscuits in the tin!'

They run like mad things. 'ATTACK! DEATH TO APRICOTS!' Héloïse yells. And Barnabé yells so as to please Héloïse. Her hand is a miracle. Barnabé wishes the corridor would never stop unfolding beneath their feet.

'Of course he's asking questions. Lots of questions! He's seven years old! Everyone in his class has a father. He'll manage to read in front of the other kids when he knows he has one. I'll tell him that.'

'Who?'

'Lawrence!'

'What about the guy from the beach? The sailor?'

'The lieutenant commander! Don't start.'

'It's the same thing.'

'Sailors are just servants – right at the bottom of the ladder! They're the guys who wash down the decks!'

'You're mad . . . You're talking about a man who doesn't exist.'

'I know! That is precisely why I am going to tell Barnabé to forget about that lieutenant commander! I'll explain to him that I couldn't talk about his real father before . . . because Lawrence is married. He has his precious reputation . . . his luxury apartment . . . his jealous little wife . . . I had to, didn't I, in the meantime? I had to come up with a father for him who'd be worthy of the name!'

'Violette?'

'You haven't the slightest clue about anything . . .'

'Is Lawrence Barnabé's father?'

'He has responsibilities! He made promises! And deep down, I'm sure it's him.'

'We've worked it out a thousand times . . . You'd been apart for six months when—'

'But didn't he come back to fuck me after we broke up? Perhaps! Like he did before, turning up at all hours! "Violette, I want to press those slutty tits of yours down really hard on the kitchen table!"'

'Did it happen or didn't it?'

'He thinks he can do whatever he likes and he'll never have to face the music.'

'Did it happen?'

'Yes, it happened! Of course it did! Or, no, it didn't happen. What difference does it make?'

Violette sits on the unmade bed beside her sister and, in the tone of a stubborn child, digs for proofs and remnants in the strata of her memory.

'In a minuscule restaurant in Tokyo . . . everyone's elbows were in each other's meals . . . I spilt soup on my brand new kimono . . . Lawrence had bought it in a shop in the hotel. It was silk with a landscape scene embroidered on it: a mountain, the peak covered in snow . . . a pagoda . . . a carp in a lake, its head poking out of the water . . . and a couple in traditional costume standing under a cherry tree next to the lake . . . The soup went all over the Japanese lady's head and Lawrence said to me: "You've tipped it all over your head . . ." He meant that they were us . . . it was him and me, the couple in front of the mountain of eternal snow . . . He was the man and I was the woman and we would love each other for ever.'

Héloïse and Barnabé are hiding inside the kitchen cupboard. They whisper inside their simulated night, kiss each other on the lips, beneath the shelves, the provisions, the jars of green-gages, the packets of ground coffee; their hands pat the biscuits in the tin, recognising shapes, leaving the club- and spade-shaped ones, picking out the heart ones, dipping them in the jam, trying to push them into the other one's mouth – who bursts into giggles, feeling the sticky biscuit exploring around their chin, nose, lips, and takes a bite leaving behind fingers covered in spit.

'Your mother sent us to the kitchen on purpose.'

'I know. It's because they want to talk about something secret.'

'They're stupid. What's the secret?'

'It's Lawrence, of course.'

'Again! They always talk about the same thing.'

'She doesn't want to tell me he's my father. So I don't get disturbed.'

'What?'

'She tells everyone: if Barnabé finds out that Lawrence is his bi-logical father, it will be a terrible shock, he'll be dread-fully upset.'

'You're lucky. He's so good looking.'

'Rubbish, he's old.'

'He's not old! He runs with trainers on in the Tuileries!'

'That doesn't prove it. Mum says he's got a midlife crisis.'

'Who's that?'

'It's when you're old.'

'Stop it, Barnabé! He's not old! He has trainers! He's the head of all the doctors in Paris! He has the Louvre pyramid in his garden!'

'It's not his garden – it's everyone's!'

'Anyway, he says I'm stoical! Later we're going to sleep together and we'll live in the pyramid.'

'You can't! It's made of glass – everyone will see you having a bath!'

'You're so thick! There must be more floors lower down! The bathroom will be in the basement!'

'Shut up, you're shouting too loud. If they hear us, they'll come and—'

'You're so annoying, Barnabé! You're always afraid!'

'He's much too old. No one can marry someone that old!'

'I won't get married, I'm just going to sleep with him.'

'I don't want you to sleep with my father!'

The cupboard door opens. Daylight, two tall mothers, one dark-haired, one blonde, hands on hips, and the kitchen bare of magic.

IV

Héloïse is sitting, straight backed, on the edge of the bed. Her head is pink, cuts show on her scalp, and she has the bloodless hue of the lit candle that stands day and night on the chest of drawers, throwing its flickering halo over the portrait of grandfather Georges in his soldier's uniform. Behind the door, a voice rises in defence of Héloïse. Violette understands her niece. She has the same ardent character, the same courage. She knows that friendship always faces its dragons and sea monsters. She blames Mirabelle and Lawrence for their lack of poetry: Héloïse should be an example to them, they should strew flowers before her, kiss the bare expanse of her head. Then she melts into sobs. Mirabelle raises her eyes to the heavens. Her sister's exorbitant romantic lunacy has always alarmed her. Violette's highly strung personality has shaped Mirabelle's complexes, her measured approach, the stubborn idea that she is the duller of the two sisters. Mirabelle has noticed that men rate Violette's craziness. What's more, she thinks that their situation exemplifies a general rule: men go for crazy women. Especially sensible men. They are seduced by the intimidating deformity of a crazy mind. Attracted by a pair of legs that might at any moment lock around their necks and strangle them. Crazy women have hair that illustrates what's inside their heads – try as they might to dye it or comb it down, it will grow back in tune with their thoughts, like spear grass. Men don't understand that what they find dazzling in the rages and joyful transports of a crazy woman is in fact their own youth. Their long lost imagination. Men worship the small of a woman's back: crazy women have a more deeply marked furrow in their lower backs because a torrent of emotions runs through their bellies and eats away at their waists. Rational men see the crazy woman's every gesture as a purposeless and perfect dance step; her unfinished sentences as secret messages. They take the crazy woman for a work of art. Mirabelle concludes to herself that, whatever the pertinence of her hypothesis, men have always preferred Violette. Mirabelle looks at her feet, at her bourgeois shoes, devoid of fantasy, funereally polished, smelling like the back of a cupboard. Lawrence and Violette: two people who really know about footwear. One elegantly casual and the other a charming eccentric, born on a boat in the middle of the Mediterranean. Mirabelle wishes she could banish her feet altogether. She is as ashamed as in her nights of anxiety, of the recurring nightmare of the Champs-Élysées, the long pedestrian crossing that she walks completely naked, the sun at its zenith, her unluckily placed beauty spot, her breasts, her bottom, the scar over her appendix, her vagina, which she cannot hide because her arms are occupied by two sleeping infants, the car horns that have her in icy sweats, the other pedestrians' stares, a man in uniform strides towards Mirabelle just as she realises that a gelatinous red trickle is dripping from her thighs and marring the white strip of the pedestrian crossing, the man in uniform who is wearing boots fitted with clappers, *clonk! clonk! clonk!,* brandishes his book of fines for, as Mirabelle knows perfectly well, the law prohibits women from sullying pedestrian crossings with their sticky menstrual blood.

She compares her feet to her sister's. Violette is wearing bright red Moroccan slippers. Violette is original. 'What a number, that one!' Jeanne always said in a tone of maternal pride and perplexed admiration that cut Mirabelle to the quick. The lounge door opens and the tree is there, the dishes laid out on the red linen, the family gathered together, as every year for St Nicholas, and, through the living room windows, at the end of the rue du Pas-de-la-Mule, the place des Vosges, the slate of those steep roofs, the facades rosy in the setting sun, the rows of lime trees, the gentleness of the lawns and Louis XIII on horseback in white marble, whom Jeanne dismisses as a mere copy, explaining that the original statue was a bronze and that 'they' – the villains' names remain a blank – had melted it down during the Revolution in order to cast cannons. Marine is carrying baby Caroline on her hip, with all her great rolls of fat, unbuttoned pyjamas and a swollen nappy showing mustard tones in the light. Lawrence, Violette and Mirabelle block the way to Jeanne's bedroom.

'Change her in the study with the red birds, rather . . . not in Jeanne's room. Héloïse is in there.'

'Is she ill?'

'She's been naughty.'

Naughty. Mirabelle imagines Baptiste's anger when he sees the bald head. Perhaps a hat or a wig. Two hours earlier, Baptiste, his bow suspended above the strings, cello gently gripped between his splayed thighs and, without looking up from his score: 'I'm not coming.' Mirabelle was standing, wearing a colourless skirt, smiling, made-up, her look completed by the hated court shoes. Under her arm she had a large book on Vermeer's paintings that she had planned to give to her mother but ended up leaving in the hallway because, while turning the pages of his score, Baptiste had said that ever since Héloïse's birth he'd been doing his best to tolerate this moronic family get-together, his mother-in-law's hypocritical looks, the over-the-top, ridiculously decorated tree, straight out of a fancy department store window display, art books pretentiously set out on coffee tables, the kids' spoilt faces all begging to be smacked, the crazy little girl getting on everyone's nerves with her nail varnish, the pretentious 'home-made' spread intended to save the cost of going to a proper caterer, the small talk about private schools, skiing holidays and the prices of ski lifts, and of course the trio of silly hens, Mirabelle, Violette and their mother Jeanne, dumbstruck and good-for-nothing in front of Lawrence, the old buck who behaves as if he's right at home, putting ornaments where they belong, popping the champagne, poking his silver sex bomb tongue up all the women in the family. Marine comes out of the red study, baby Caroline on her hip, the dirty nappy held tightly in one hand. Lawrence leans over to kiss the baby's nose.

'You all look as though someone's died . . . What is it?' (Marine, who has always lived in France, has, out of love, caught her father's Irish accent.)

Lawrence says that Héloïse has shaved her head, shaved off her beautiful curly hair, in solidarity with Barnabé, who has lice and can't get rid of them. Mirabelle wonders if Baptiste will be asleep when they get back. A wig. Finding a wigmaker. Finding a wigmaker that's open on a Sunday evening. When

Baptiste is not pleased, he hits out (at Mirabelle, the walls and doors, the lid of the grand piano). He won't be able to stand this bareheaded daughter. He will think of those women after the war. Through the open door of the living room, Violette can see the troubled outline of Barnabé sprawled on the chaise longue, his nails frenetically working at his scalp full of dirty creatures.

The night before, Violette had taken him to a restaurant for his birthday.

'How is it being ten?'

'Dunno.'

'It's exciting to be a round number!'

'Why's it exciting?'

Tongue sticking out, Barnabé licked the icy taste of artificial vanilla off his spoon.

'Will you tell me about *papa*?'

'But my Barnabubble . . . you know everything already! I've told you a hundred times! I met your father on a beach in Toulon . . . It was beautiful weather for March. You know all this . . .'

'Tell it again.'

'All right: he was a marine officer . . . A lieutenant commander to be precise . . . Very tall, very handsome, the strong and silent type . . . like Gary Cooper.'

'Who's he?'

'Only the greatest actor of all time! Your father had a dimple in the middle of his chin . . . And what else . . . He smoked a pipe! He loved going to auctions!'

'How do you know?'

'He told me.'

'He said: "I love going to auctions"?'

'Oh – and he had a little moustache! Just like your granddad Georges . . . Wait. I'll show you a photo of your grandfather . . .'

Violette whipped from her purse one half of a photograph taken in the garden in Oran in 1945. All smiles, Georges was posing on one knee to the left of a fabulously boxy cactus decked with black gems. To the right of the cactus, before a furious Jeanne had snipped her off, had stood Ouarda, Mirabelle's Algerian nanny.

'You see, that's the greenhouse where my father used to do his botanical experiments . . . and at the back, a corner of the house where Mirabelle and my parents used to live . . . I wasn't born yet . . . I was born on a boat . . .'

'I know.'

'My father is at least fifty in this photo. He was much older than *maman*. . . And, d'you see that moustache? The same as your father's!'

'And after the beach, you went to the restaurant with the crocodile bags?'

'It was the fanciest restaurant in Toulon! All the women had diamond necklaces and crocodile handbags . . .'

'Real crocodile?'

'Of course! And real diamonds! All the men were wearing bow ties. We even drank a bottle of wine that cost 400 francs! And then, the next morning, your father set sail again.'

'And what did you do during the night?'

'Well my darling . . . we made you.'

'How did you make me?'

'We just did . . . You know . . . Without thinking . . . And wait . . . His name was Martin, but did you know you had to say it like Martine? Because he was from Ireland, like Lawrence,' said Violette, looking down at the vanilla ice cream that had completely melted in Barnabé's bowl.

'Why did he go away again?'

'He had no choice, my Boububble! His boat was leaving for India or China . . . I've forgotten the details, my darling . . .'

Barnabé looked into his spoon at the reflection of his face distorted by Violette's stories. Every year the legend gained two or three brand new details. This time it was the moustache, Gary Cooper and the dimple in the middle of the chin.

Barnabé is scratching so hard that his scalp bleeds. Violette sees herself as she was ten years earlier, sat on that same chaise longue, with Barnabé's mouth at her breast. He has become a little man and the chaise longue has had a change of costume. Jeanne has replaced the elegant stripes with a yellow-and-royal-blue Provençal print, loud, inappropriate both for Paris and for the curves of the aspirational chaise longue. It's intended to recall the curtains in Marseille and the tresses of garlic pinned to the kitchen beams (or so Jeanne claims). Never once did Violette see, in that bare, colourless Marseille apartment, penetrated sparingly by the sun through the half-open shutters, the least little rag of Provençal print. The copper pans were never used but hung in order from the largest to the smallest above the black oak table. The coffee mill, the scale with its weights likewise stacked heaviest to lightest, the bare monk's table, the green bird, its cage, its sad song, the patches of sunlight on the empty walls. And Jeanne on the bench in the hallway, in floods of tears, her shopping between her feet.

*

Mirabelle thinks: *The hair that Héloïse has slashed off – that's me. Flesh of my flesh. Hair of my hair.* She tugs at Lawrence's sleeve.

'Tell her it's very serious . . . that people will be horrified . . . that her head will frighten them . . . that her father . . . Tell her he'll be angry. And tell her also that it'll never grow back like before . . . that she looks like a cancer patient . . . No, don't tell her that! Just tell her that she always knows how to make me ashamed in front of everyone.'

'Your Héloïse has always had a talent for excess.'

Violette is shocked. *Always had a talent for excess.* That's exactly what Lawrence said to her on the night of the birth, on seeing the fish scale dress and the jewellery at her neck, wrists and ankles, jingling into the slowly snowing sky. Has Lawrence forgotten that he said the same thing to her? Does he not have even one memory of them left? (And if so, which? When their bid won at the auction in Tokyo, the Muromachi painting, and she had given him a blowjob in the men's toilets beside the auction room? When, in the restaurant, he had presented her with a road sign, an enormous, heavy – real – one, stolen from the forest in Fontainebleau, that read 'Beware: Riders Crossing'?)

As he comes in, Lawrence breathes in the scent of lavender and clean laundry. Héloïse puts her hands flat on her head.

'Don't look.'

Lawrence sits down on the battered, old, woollen mattress that Jeanne refuses to replace and kisses her head between two blonde tufts that have escaped the razor.

'When I was your age, little lion, I came to Paris with my father, Laoghaire. He was not . . . not an easy kind of guy; he didn't talk much. He had been invited to the Sorbonne. He

40

was Professor of Semantics at Trinity College, Dublin. That means he taught his students about the meaning of words. And for a man who was incapable of saying a word to his wife and children, well, I've always found that frustrating . . . odd, you know . . . this passion for language . . . We crossed the whole of the Celtic Sea and part of the Channel . . . Laoghaire told me that I was going to see *liberated Paris* – I didn't dare ask *from what* . . . And then I knew that if I said one more word, I would be sick all over the bridge of the boat . . . It was the end of the war, my little lion . . . Paris liberated from the Germans . . . We docked, I don't remember where . . . at Cherbourg, I think . . . We took a train as far as Paris and when we got out of the train, there was this woman . . . twenty-five years old . . . and six or seven guys who were having a great time pushing her about on the platform. They were tossing her between them like a ball, from one to the next . . . She was like a rag doll . . . she let them do it . . . She had swastikas on her cheeks and her blouse was torn right through – it was the first time I saw breasts . . . She was shaven; they had shaved her hair off. People were stopping to look. My father said that the woman had tried to make her country lose the war . . . But his voice was shaking and he held my hand tight . . . And then a man jostled me, he pushed through the crowd, went up to the girl and shook her by both arms . . . He said: "I've lost two sons, you Bosch-loving whore . . ." I didn't understand anything . . . and you don't either, my little lion, you don't understand. He said that he knew the girl's parents . . . He began yelling her name: "France Sauveur . . ."'

V

Héloïse turns the pages of the natural science manual: the
yellow spores on the undersides of fern fronds, the sea
urchin's five orange gonads, the red fly agarics with their
white spots, and the feeling that everything is sexual. To
Mirabelle's question through the half-open door, Héloïse
replies: 'No, I already know it all by heart.' Mirabelle folds
the threadbare, faded, pink towel embroidered with her
daughter's initials over the bidet. Carefully places the farm
animals and jointed figurines around the edge of the bath.
While she lines up the farmer, the farmer's wife, the three-
legged sheep, the chicken, the horse and her foal, Mirabelle
wonders, with a pang, if Héloïse has not grown too old for
toys in the bath.

On the other side of the wall, Héloïse undresses, oblivious
to the row of elephants marching trunk to tail along the
wallpaper. She inspects the unattractive new growth on her
head in the long mirror. The pair of knickers tossed across the
bedroom comes to rest on the head of a doll whose hairdo
has not been touched for the last two years. Héloïse looks at
herself. In the centre of her own prehistoric egg, her smooth,
rounded pubis, she sees one long, dark hair. Mirabelle and
Héloïse have dinner in almost complete silence. Baptiste plays

a Bach sarabande, shut away in his study. He replays the same few bars over and over. Each performance is followed by a deep exhalation in the same fashion as the music: austere and melancholy.

'Are you ready for your test? Sure you don't want to recite it for me?'

Héloïse's smile of refusal is so mature and serene that Mirabelle feels like crying. (*I shan't set up the farm animals around the bath any more.*)

'We'll have to change your wallpaper one of these days . . . The elephants all trunk to tail; you're a bit too grown-up for them now, don't you think?'

'Oh no, Mummy! It reminds me of when I was little!'

Mirabelle grits her teeth. She is being robbed. Héloïse's contented mouth at her breast: robbed. Héloïse busy with her wooden ovens and doll's house pots and pans: robbed. Héloïse overjoyed at the tower of cubes as tall as herself, Héloïse in tears before the fallen tower, Héloïse curled up asleep without a seatbelt, adorably pretty on the back seat of the Renault 5.

The next day, Héloïse drags Barnabé into the maelstrom of the boulevards. When you're playing truant, every minute overflows with time. Lawrence, on the corner of the street. He is wearing a little pink-and-black checked hat. A woman beside him in a dress as pale as her neck and wrists.

'Camille, let me introduce you to two rascals who have escaped from school . . . This grown-up girl is Héloïse, whom I've known since she was a baby . . . and her cousin . . .'

'Barnabé.' (Says Barnabé.)

'And this is Camille who, under my benevolent supervision,

44

is writing an excellent doctoral thesis all about pain in severe burns patients.'

Camille smiles, arms crossed; shy, something of her escapes them.

'I've caught you red-handed, Héloïse! Have you nothing to say for yourself? Your mother will be beside herself with worry!'

The voice is undermined by an unusually strong Irish accent. Camille looks down. Lawrence raps out the syllables with stiff little taps on Héloïse's cheek, and she feels her heart leap out of her chest and dance a waltz there on the pavement.

'Which of you two is going to explain what you've been getting up to here?'

Barnabé blames Héloïse. He hadn't wanted to follow her. It was her idea. All their ideas were her ideas. Since they had sneaked out of the school doors, Barnabé has been thinking about the test on ferns and fungi, about the letter of excuse they'd have to make up, about forging Violette's signature. Héloïse is thrilled. She flies in the face of danger.

'We're playing at getting rich.'

Héloïse wants to explain the rules of their game but the effect that her unfinished explanation produces in Lawrence delights her: he has that marvelling inward smile that she has caught on his face before. Camille lights a cigarette.

Camille is better known as Margaux. She was once a student of Fleur's; Fleur has already coaxed her arm into a smoother curve, lifted her chin, said: 'Imagine that a thread is drawing you up from the top of your head towards heaven.'

Margaux is a dancer at the Opéra and a vegetarian – she is even planning to stop eating eggs. She has never been in love. She lives with Louise XIII, her cat. She says it is time for her to take retirement and Lawrence loves hearing her say 'my retirement', three imaginary wrinkles at the corners of her eyes. Margaux would like to teach dance to eight-year-olds who haven't yet been conditioned in any way, little girls to be moulded and shaped. Eight – that's the golden age. Time is slowly killing Margaux, bit by bit. First the sexless, fairy form evaporated along with the last mists of childhood. Her skin lost its smooth glow. Her hair darkened, her cheeks grew thinner. Her voice left the limpid high notes behind. Then came breasts, hair, hips and blood. After making love, Margaux sits and anxiously examines the surface of her body for the villainous tracks of time.

'Look, Lawrence!'

She is holding the soft, elastic skin of her belly in her fist. She pulls at it.

'It's your belly.'

'It's not funny! I didn't use to have a belly.'

Lawrence allows an indulgent glance to sweep over his own body. The hairs on his chest are turning to ash and snow.

'Yes you did; you have always had a belly. Thank God.'

Margaux prefers men who go into ecstasies over her body and beg her for the secret of her incredible youthfulness. She does not like Lawrence's irony. He does not admire her. Margaux purposely skips away rather than walking. Lawrence watches her there on the clean bathroom tiles. Childish ways. She won't let adulthood in. Lawrence likes Margaux's wide mouth. The rest, dry and muscular, reminds him of a dance exercise. He thinks of Fleur's body which, despite the years of tyrannical dance, has always been feminine.

'Let's go back! They'll murder us!'

'What for, Bébé? The test began ages ago . . .'

'Lawrence will tell your mum and my mum!'

'He won't say anything, Bébé . . .'

'Stop calling me Bébé.'

'Don't get angry, Barnabé . . . If you stay, I'll let you see.'

'You always say that.'

'This time, I will.'

'On the street?'

'No, over there, in the square. Behind the slides, there's a hut with a door that opens and closes.'

'Does it lock?'

'We can wedge it with a stick or our feet.'

'Do you swear?'

'I swear, Bébé.'

'On whose life?'

'On Lawrence's life.'

Barnabé smiles despite the coercion. He often dreams that he's walking at Lawrence's side in the midst of the Barbary figs, down a long, winding path at Sciroccu, his grandmother's house in Corsica. The sea is waiting, fresh and new, like a blank page of unvarying, impossible blue. Lawrence listens, Barnabé throws caution to the winds, Barnabé says in a great rush that goes off-track bit by bit: 'I know that you were with my mother and that you had a child and that that child is me so you must be no not must but well it's natural isn't it but I'm not expecting anything I'm not angry I'm not sad and I don't miss you and even if I was born oh don't worry I'm not going to call you *papa*.'

Héloïse takes two teaspoons from her pocket.

'You should have got some money from your mother's bag.'

'This game doesn't need money, Bébé.'

'We won't get far with a couple of spoons.'

'I'm going far.'

They synchronise their watches.

'We meet in front of the merry-go-round in two hours.'

'Two hours? What about maths . . .'

'Bébé, stop fussing.'

Héloïse goes over the rules of the game. It is forbidden to steal. It is forbidden to buy anything. The aim is to bring back the most extraordinary object they can. The craziest and the most beautiful. They wish each other good luck and head off in opposite directions. Barnabé walks away purposefully, with confidence: Héloïse might turn around to look at him, so his walk must not betray the truth (fear of getting lost and diffidence).

She has drawn a red mouth where her lips used to be. Barnabé has chosen her because she is old, not in a hurry, and she is waiting for the bus, decorously, a plastic bag from the patisserie at the end of her hideously thin sleeve.

'We're doing a project, the kids in my class . . .'

'I'm not deaf! So stop shouting!'

'I'm not shouting, but since you're elderly . . . Anyway, it's a project about savings, you see . . . Everyone is going around the city with a spoon . . .'

'Well now. The days are long gone when one learned things at school.'

'. . . and the aim of the project is for each student to exchange their spoon for an object of greater value, then do it again, and again, so as to become rich as Croesus by the end of the day. Do you see?'

The old lady bursts out laughing. One gold tooth. She snatches the spoon out of Barnabé's hand and from her plastic bag takes a pretty *Patisserie Gaultier* box tied with a ribbon.

'Here you go, young man. I loathe orange-flavoured chocolates! I don't know how to make Jeanne-Marie understand how much I hate orange chocolates! Citrus and chocolate – aaaaargh! Unnatural combination! Oranges and cocoa don't even grow on the same continent! She is such a clot, Jeanne-Marie!'

Barnabé is growing impatient. The horses and carriages go round and round in a dizzying spin of gilded mouldings, flashing bulbs and creaking barrel organ. He cracks the joints of each finger in turn. Background noise of a skeleton. Héloïse is a minute late – on Barnabé's wrist the second hand stops moving when you look at it. He has spent two hours knocking on doors – and the more doors that opened to him, the happier and more excited he became. Shopkeepers, passersby, customers, American tourists – Barnabé has used his patter on half of Paris. He feels in his pocket for the stone the colour of a well-sucked violet cough sweet. The jeweller gave him the amethyst in exchange for a whisky service, brand new, with a Bohemian crystal decanter and two matching, hand-cut

glasses. In the basement of the Bazar de l'Hôtel de Ville department store, at the 'returns and exchanges' counter, a furious
woman had explained to Barnabé that the whisky service was
a wedding present from her good-for-nothing bum of a
brother-in-law, a notorious alcoholic, and that, in order to go
ahead with the reimbursement, the saleswoman was
demanding the receipt, which obviously she was unable to
produce, seeing as it was rotting in the pocket of the inebri-
ated brother-in-law who was passed out fully dressed in some
random bed, or under a bridge, that she detested aperitifs
and digestifs, that she thoroughly mistrusted men who
enjoyed them and that she, on the other hand, adored Marcel
Proust, whose work she had never read to be completely
honest, but her sister (the alcoholic's wife) said that he was
the greatest writer and that once you'd read him you could
forget the rest of these literary also-rans. Hence Barnabé's
proposal to exchange a three-volume 1947 edition of *À la
recherche du temps perdu* with seventy-seven illustrations by Van
Dongen for the whisky service could not have come at a better
moment. Barnabé had obtained this damp-spotted publica-
tion, smelling of black earth, oak roots and mushrooms that
had sprung up overnight, in exchange for a Swiss cuckoo clock
that had made Monsieur Fledermaus's blue eyes shine,
hunched and shrunken as he was beneath the stacks of treasures in his curiosity shop. When the hour struck an ostrich
would shoot out of a chalet door. This peculiarity inspired the
soon-to-be centenarian antique dealer to say that of all life's
emotions, wonder was his favourite. As for the cuckoo clock,
Barnabé was given this in exchange for the orange chocolates,
from the hands of a red-haired old lady in a wedding dress,

hollering that she had gone to Bavaria hoping to bring Hans-Jakob back in the nick of time.

Stepping out of the jeweller's shop, Barnabé knows that he has the most extraordinary object. In the flashes of light cast by the merry-go-round, Barnabé silently compliments himself. He has not cheated. He has confronted strangers and not friendly ones either. He has turned lead into gold. The teaspoon has become a purple gemstone. A smile transforms his lips. They'll go to the shed. Héloïse will show him. Is it wet like a tongue? Is it deep? Is it true that looking at it in full daylight can make you go blind? (Surely not, that's stupid.) Is it true that sometimes there are thorns on the inside? (Possibly.) Héloïse's vagina.

It is too late for the shed, for the sexual thorns. Héloïse never keeps her promises. The merry-go-round goes round. The children blur round before their mothers, waving their arms. Barnabé looks at the little faces that, with every turn, replay the same show of irrepressible love. And the mothers never wearying of it. Are they pretending to be happy? Héloïse must have given up. She went to school. Or perhaps she lay down in the sweet grass of the Place des Vosges, between the hooves of Louis XIII's horse. But here she is running across the square pavement in front of St Paul's Church. She has lost the elastic band that held back her hair, now filled with wind and, in her graceful, generous arms, a black African panther, stuffed and mounted, muzzle forced wide open by its growl.

VI

Exhausted, unmoving, lying full length on the jetty after lunch, Héloïse, one foot in the Mediterranean, precious stones at the wavelets' crests, deadly calm shimmering, crimson nails, black sunglasses, mouth half open, cherry-red, sensual mint syrup, drops of water running down the glass, tongue running over lips, belly button rising and sinking with each deep breath in the vacant heat of July, little red briefs, a minimal bathing costume bought that morning at the market in Cargèse, scorching scent of the scrub, hair bleached by direct sunlight and sea salt, spread out, angelically, on the white towel, a rectangle of snow in the slow, silent furnace of the siesta hour, adolescent legs, transparent golden down, arms extended as if to yawn, armpit with sweat pearling, breasts, barely, sexual swelling of the pink tips pointing into the blue of the almost immaculate sky, a single cloud hanging above the far side of the bay, lightly whipped cotton, Tahitian coconut oil sun lotion, mahogany-fitted speedboat moored to the jetty, perfection of her neck, polished shoulders, two pebbles in the living swell, rosemary breeze, wicked shadows between Héloïse's relaxed thighs, parted in extravagance and by her hand slipped in between, midnight-green parasol pines silhouetted against the sky of her thirteenth summer.

From the shade of the eucalyptus, Lawrence is observing her, basking red and bare-skinned on her towel. He holds a straw hat by the brim. *The Great Gatsby* open on the deckchair. White linen trousers. Buttoned flies. Tight and hard. Nausea around his temples. Influx of blood. Blossoming white blotches in the over-exposed landscape. Legs of wet clay. Hand flat on the ragged trunk of the eucalyptus. Wedding ring gleaming on his left ring finger. Fainting as he looks into those poisonous thighs.

Héloïse calls for help. Violette taps the fleshy part of Lawrence's cheeks so as not to hurt him, administers bizarre entreaties, loving nicknames and insults. And, as Lawrence remains unconscious, Fleur gives him an abrupt slap in the face. Nosebleed. Lawrence's daughters, Justine and Marine, twenty-four and twenty-five years old, scream in unison, at exactly the same pitch. Violette pulls out a handkerchief – Mirabelle does as well, but is too late – to plug the nostril. Four little discs of blood on the limestone paving. Violette says that Jeanne will be furious: Jeanne is still having her afternoon coffee on the terrace, looking out to the sea; she will notice the blood on the white stone straight away; we'll be hearing about it until next summer, or the one after, until the rain and the wind have cleaned away the last red globule. Lawrence opens his eyes: red monokini. Héloïse.

'*Papa*? Can you see me?'

'Very well.'

'You collapsed on the terrace . . . You had a turn.'

54

'No!'

'Shall I call the doctor?'

'I *am* the doctor, my dear . . .'

'*Papa!* You frightened us all!'

'A touch of sunstroke . . . really nothing to worry about . . .'

'But you were in the shade.'

They surround him: Mirabelle, Violette, Fleur, Justine, Marine, Héloïse, a chorus of worried women. Even the gardener Ange, a pair of secateurs hanging from one hand, is looking at him strangely. Baptiste comes down the stone steps behind Barnabé, who is blossoming into adolescence at an animal pace, his acrobat's physique enhanced by a deep, gold tan.

'Is he bleeding?' (Baptiste is asking; he's annoyed.)

'Not because of passing out . . . It was Fleur . . . She hit him . . .' (Violette's speech is interrupted by her thudding heart.)

'Excuse me, Violette, but your motherly patting and affectionate words were not doing much to bring him round.'

'My what?'

'"My panther! My angel! My hellfire!"' (Fleur is venomous.)

'I'm sorry I was concerned upon finding your husband half dead on the ground!'

'Quite right, Violette. Do concern yourself about my husband.'

Fleur escapes down the steps edged with sour fig, oleanders, rosemary and neatly coiffed clumps of lavender – three butterflies are arguing over one mauve spike. Fleur is roaring with laughter, mad laughter. The rope soles of her espadrilles bounce lightly on the blinding surface of the steps. She has not danced for years but her ankles remember her ballet shoes. Knowing nothing of weight, her ethereal body floats above the garden; invisible threads draw her up to the tops of the pine trees.

Violette is stretched out on the deckchair, Lawrence's straw hat lying on her stomach. She notices two bruises on Mirabelle's forearm and instantly looks away, her head stubbornly blank, at Barnabé, balancing on the stump of the hundred-year-old pine brought down by lightning the summer before, creating an uncanny blaze amid the deluge of rain. Violette recognises the wide forehead of the baby that was born while she slept, through the skin of her cut-open belly. Caesarian. Baby born like Julius Caesar. He is handsome, she is proud, she loves him and her love has seen them through it all. Barnabé sees Héloïse on the beach below, in a gesture of modesty and self-exhibition, covering her beginnings of breasts with her palms. Barnabé's stomach twists at the mere sight of her looking at Lawrence. Héloïse watches Lawrence's body enter the water, slowly, brown spots scattered on his broad back by the sun, marks of age. Lawrence isn't looking at anyone, or perhaps only at the sea monster, half-woman, half-killer whale, on the horizon's lip.

Héloïse is walking, she is looking, joyously, hurriedly, for her sandals, left somewhere. The stone paths zigzag between the agaves and the Barbary figs, abductors lying in nocturnal ambush, ready to catch her wrist, scratch her mouth, tear her dress so as to touch her breasts, ready to hear her breathing echo the immense breathing of the black pines, the fluting call of a scops owl, the voice of the night pale with stars. At the end of the garden the paved footpath becomes a steep, roughly hewn track descending among the rockrose and broom all the way to the beach where the sea melts into a black sky, indivisible, pierced by the arc of moon drawing a milky ladder along its surface. Héloïse hurtles down the track; barefoot in the cool sand, she walks softly, more slowly. She can see nothing of the figure approaching except for the glowing, orange-red spark of a cigarette.

'I've lost my sandals.'

'Have you seen the moon in the water?'

'A thorn cut my foot on the way . . . I thought I left them outside after dinner, under the table.'

Lawrence tries to make her out in the darkness. He has thrown his cigarette away.

'What are you doing here?'

'We said we'd meet.'

'You and me?'

'You said midnight.'

'I was joking, my little lion.'

'Why? Because you're going out with Fleur?'

'I'm not *going out* with Fleur – I'm married to Fleur! Tomorrow it'll be twenty-six years. Will you help me make her a cake?'

'Is it 'cos you're married that you don't want to?'

'No, it's because you're twelve years old.'

'Thirteen.'

'Go back to bed, my lionnessy.'

'You fancy me.' (Héloïse has guts.)

'You should be more wary of other people . . . It's night time . . . You go out, all—'

'Say you don't fancy me.'

'Of course I don't fancy you. An adult couldn't fancy you. Héloïse, I swear to you that you will be so beautiful—'

'You get hard when you look at me.'

'No.' (Lawrence's voice sounds different.) 'You think you want to do something that, in your heart, you don't really want to do.'

'What?'

'What have you come here for?'

'Love.' (She is serious and 'love' cracks in her throat.)

'Héloïse, this isn't funny.'

'It's you who's changed your mind. I've been wanting to since I was born.'

Héloïse puts her hand on her tummy. Lawrence watches the fingers crumple the fabric of her dress, looks up at her fierce eyes, her face silver in the moonlight.

'Lawrence . . .'

'My sweet lion.'

'Are you looking at me?'

Héloïse sheds her dress. She lets her skimpy knickers drop right down her thighs and calves. She has make-up on. She is naked; all he can see is her red mouth. Her vagina tightens and relaxes. When Héloïse thinks about Lawrence, in bed, in the bath, in public toilets, she makes her clitoris swell with minute strokes of her index finger and, in the same way, her vagina tightens and relaxes. Lawrence wonders if a whole life can be sacrificed for a pleasure already soured by cruelty and melancholy, even before it is savoured. He steps forward, touches the tiny waist, the knob of her spine and the buttocks that a shiver of apprehension has covered with goose bumps. The softness of the breasts, hardly begun, the hips recoil as he touches the pubis, the fine hair, the wet lips, and the finger, the whole middle finger inside the sex tight with fear and pleasure, the sex which has never been penetrated except by felt tips, the shaft of a spoon, a small statue of St Thérèse of Lisieux and a stick of glue.

Lawrence is walking the highwire. On either side: the abyss and death; but balancing on the wire, the marvellous body, the mouth new to kissing, the tongue and its channel of saliva on his Adam's apple, the hairs spiralling down the torso, the soft tummy, the cock only now remembering that it could stiffen so brutally and painfully, the balls that had never, that they could recall, ever been so slowly, exquisitely, confusedly licked.

Lawrence strokes Héloïse's hair. She knows nothing and she knows everything. Beginners' luck. *I have deflowered the little lion.* He thinks it to himself. You never forget the first time. She was called Treesha. An Irish cousin, from County Donegal, a little older than he, come to spend the last of the year 1952 in Paris. Used to sleep in his younger sisters Brenna and Orghlaith's bedroom. The smell of seaweed at low tide in her vagina that was sixteen concupiscent Mays old. She wanted both to have the penis enter her and for it not to move, *don't move Lawrence*, and to have her nipples pinched, very hard, harder, *harder Lawrence!*, and with a thumb in her arse, but *decently*, and kissed on the neck, but *without tickling*, and her breasts licked but *without dribbling*. A discouragement. Sudden qualms at the height of their lovemaking, when, at last, right inside her very hairy vagina. 'Lawrence, I think we're doing a bad thing.' Treesha full of remorse, talking, without believing in them, of the devil and damnation. Fits of weeping. And as if to rebuke Lawrence, his cousin pointed at the gouts of semen on the flowery bedspread. *Dirty milk* she called it, with an ambiguous smile. Disgusting milk. Uncontrollable erections in the bathroom when she ordered him to watch her undress, but *not thinking about anything* to slide the soap over her body, but *not going here or here*, and to call her, in a low voice so that Mrs Calvagh would not hear, a dirty sow and little slut, but *not thinking it for real*. A haunted, tormented adolescent. Her kisses, still: a simple, perfect sanctuary. Sweet, long, tasting of Coca-Cola. Treesha used to smile like a shy girl during family lunches. When she left the Calvaghs' home, Lawrence's father had only one word for her: hussy.

Héloïse slides both hands around Lawrence's hips, and he finds himself counting the years. He will be sixty when she is twenty. He'll be snuffing it on the stroke of eighty when she, in the happy valley of middle age, will be celebrating her fortieth. Mid-calculation, he realises that Héloïse is sucking an extraordinary part of his body, that he is stopping himself from coming, that not one woman in fifty-three years has yet had the erotic courtesy to lick his arsehole. They surface. Tears. He is filled with the fear of dying never having been able – despite a loving family, achievements, islands of passion – to be unreservedly happy.

Héloïse stands up, her lips shining with saliva.

'Was it nice or not?'

He wonders how to see her again in Paris. Will her parents allow her to visit friends? In the afternoon? Night – don't even consider it. Will she make him suffer, leave him for a baby of fifteen with strange skin, some tall kid with a squeaky voice? Will it be, in the end, like all the other times? After the fever, the overwhelming power and belief, the energy and pornography of the first chapter of a passion, will there come moments of boredom, silences, a stupid, insidious comment, inferior skin, someone new?

Meeting at the hotel. The horrified face of the proprietor who gives them the room key, shaking with fury at her desk. Jealousy! Her husband hasn't looked at her in donkey's years. A brand new dress? Bernard frowns but he won't see the dress. A new pair of smart shoes? It's been fifteen years since Bernard has glanced down at Jacqueline's feet. New haircut, symmetrical curls, auburn tint? Bernard hazards a bit of pure guesswork: 'You've done something to your hair?' Bernard no longer looks at his wife and he isn't even cheating on her. Abandoned – for no other woman. For her birthday, he bought her a raincoat. Humiliation. Two sizes too small. He was thinking of the twenty-year-old Jacqueline. Belt made for an hourglass figure. Whereas these days Jacqueline has the waist of a pig, or a cabbage, or of a home-grown squash. Behind the reception desk, beside the board with the keys, the mirror mocks her, like some young slut in a micro miniskirt, standing in a nightclub doorway, with her sexy arse right in Jacqueline's face, tramping all over her varicose veins with her stiletto heels. A savage blow, filthy mirror. Face in the act of collapse. Bags under her eyes and a double chin. The hairs of a moustache. She runs hands heavy with gold rings over her loose, flabby cheeks. No memory of the last kiss that mouth received – Bernard's moustache always has left-over crumbs or sauce in

61

it. And now, in walks this arrogant fellow, handsome with his hint of Irish accent, who thinks he can treat all women of fifty like fossilised cabbage! Who smiles! Who is not ashamed to ask for a room 'for only a short while'! Who lays his hand on the little idiot's shoulder, on the unblemished body of this child destined for the ease of home and gardening, provided that life smiles on her and that enough money flows into her husband's pocket for them to buy a bit of land, to grow some vegetables and a rhododendron border! Lawrence drops the idea of the hotel the second he feels Héloïse's tongue push into his arsehole. He will rent an apartment for their meetings. He smiles into the darkness.

'I've been in love with you since I was born.'

(*Me too, my little lion.*)

Lawrence has often thought back to that summer of Héloïse at thirteen, the labyrinth of pulsing cacti, their two hearts squeezed between the parasol pines, the irreversible path, the beach white and pink in the sun, black and complicit in the starlight, overlooked by a tumbledown Genoese tower, the smuggled kisses. Héloïse. The old dry stone walled house where Mirabelle and Violette spent all their childhood holidays, and where Lawrence used to come every year with Fleur, Marine and Justine, mixing up the two families until even their memories were jumbled together. The facade with the bougainvillea and trumpet creeper, adorned with terraces and half-open white shutters. The outside staircase leading, at siesta hour, to the first floor bedrooms and the salamander above Héloïse's bed. How did they not see? How did Barnabé, the jealous lover, not see? Violette, the other jealous lover? Justine and Marine, the jealous children? Grandmother Jeanne, with her talent for fortune telling? Fleur, with her long lost illusions? The beach? The wooden jetty? The pebbles splashed with *dirty milk*? How is it that none of these snitched on them? Lies from morning to night. During the affair with Violette, Fleur said to Lawrence: 'Make an effort to tell me your best lies.' But that summer, Fleur seemed to see nothing.

In the middle of a meal, Héloïse gets up. Lawrence stands at the same moment, his accent much too Irish as soon as he begins to lie: 'Why, we're out of rosé, I'll get another bottle.' And on the table, clear as day, an untouched bottle of rosé. The lovers are less and less afraid. Something is protecting them. Perhaps the gulf of time between them, or the purity of childhood.

At the end of the summer, Mirabelle opens a bedroom door and catches, or does not catch, Lawrence relinquishing Héloïse's lips, straightening up beside the bed. 'I've been looking everywhere for you, Lawrence . . .' And Héloïse, her tone forced but with genuine concern: 'Have you had an argument with *papa*?' Mirabelle hides her face in her hands, she is going to cry and try not to cry, while Héloïse and Lawrence exchange looks – did you see that? She didn't see anything. A narrow escape.

The white linen trousers – Lawrence still has an erection. He leaves the bedroom, Mirabelle follows. Héloïse thrusts her hand into her knickers, slips her fingers one by one into her vagina. That morning he said: 'Make yourself come.'

'What?'

'Touch yourself while I look.'

Lawrence calls 'touching' what Héloïse has always called 'playing volcanoes'. This means rubbing the tumid nub with her fingers, slowing down when it grows, heats, hardens, gets aroused, rubbing harder when it dwindles and recedes, accelerating up to get to the black hole and the spasms of eruption. The animal fire and the joy in the soles of her feet, running up into her sex, the ring of her arse, the base of her skull. When she was little, on the way back from the Robert-Koch Paediatric Hospital, Héloïse played volcanoes in her cot, thinking again of Lawrence and how he had tenderly sewn, tenderly tied, tenderly touched her blood. One summer they had all gone out in a speedboat, the whole household out for the day, to the foot of Capo Rosso. Héloïse had described the volcano game to Lawrence's elder daughter who, despite being twenty, had never heard of this game for making molten lava and shaking. Then Héloïse had confided in Marine's younger sister, who knew the game well and even played it in the metro, through her tights, without anyone seeing, or perhaps they did see. 'I sit down right opposite a well-dressed man who looks like he has a wife and children and who has a leather or fake leather briefcase. He swallows, he pretends to be tightening his watch strap, but he is looking at my pussy.' Héloïse told Barnabé last. He had said that she was making things up again, that you couldn't get hot, shake and go crazy only from touching your skin. Then he had begged Héloïse to show him how she went about playing the game.

Héloïse takes her hand out of her knickers, licks her fingers, jumps off the bed and pushes the shutters wide so as to see the pines, the wooden jetty, the speedboat on the glittering, turquoise and dark blue sea, home to eels and black sea urchins. Héloïse imagines that this must be it: beauty. So she beams out into the beauty – and it looks back at her intact, a flat echo. *I wish the beauty of the landscape would flow right into me. I want to feel how beautiful it is.* The sea, the scrub clinging to the hills, the pines that sway to a jazz melody, the little white cumulus clouds. Any other landscape is equally beautiful. A vacuum cleaner factory in China, a supermarket surrounded by car parks bordered by great caterpillars of interlinked shopping trolleys, a motorway service station with its picnic tables and benches, the Robert-Koch Paediatric Hospital. Héloïse debates the question. Of course the white stone paths are stunning, flooded with sunlight, winding between purple lavender bushes all the way to the sea. For the first time, Héloïse guesses that Lawrence is suppressing all of life's emotions for the sake of one supreme emotion.

Mirabelle has always been given the same bedroom with a view over parched grassland, an abandoned sheepfold with goats befuddled by the heat, a fig tree and a wire enclosure which, despite extensive tears, has never inspired the ruminants with any inclination towards liberty – in forty years Mirabelle has seen only one escape attempt. The revolutionary goat regretted her foolhardiness and dallied behind the fence, eyes fixed on her sensible sisters, ignorant of their destiny, nibbling at the tufts of sun-seared grass. 'View with goats,' said Jeanne, promising her daughter a room with a sea view as soon as she reached the age of reason – which Jeanne fixed at thirteen, not at seven like most other parents. Jeanne felt that allowing a girl to have a sea view too young would incite too much emotion and risk making her too adventurous: an explorer, an artist, a woman of ambition, a man. Mirabelle loved her room. The grey and blue flowery curtains, the matching bedspread, what her mother called the monks' bench and on which Mirabelle used to picture a row of Franciscan brothers in brown habits, old and fat, singing *Fleur de Paris* by Maurice Chevalier. Mirabelle preferred her view with goats to any sea view. It was the indiscreet side of the house. Mirabelle had often caught sight of a boy, a shepherd on his days off – as all his days seemed to be – leaning against the trunk of the fig tree, who would pin a blade of grass between his thumbs and blow across it, trying to mimic the cock's crowing. When successful, he would spit from between his teeth, a disgusting great spurt that fascinated Mirabelle. When he failed, he would quickly look around, like a sparrow on the alert, to check, while keeping his cool, that Mirabelle was still there, leaning on her windowsill, watching him, keeping her cool. Then he would clasp his hands together into a shell shape and blow between his thumbs – it sounded like the ululation of an owl. That one worked every time, unlike the sound of the cockerel, which was more temperamental. The shepherd boy – Mirabelle never knew his name – had close-cropped hair that grew low on his neck and gormless pigeon eyes, blank but for the fear of being gobbled up by a bigger bird. But Mirabelle pretended to find him charming, an exotic specimen of Corsican mystery. She declared that he was gifted (at singing, holding his breath, writing love letters, harpoon fishing). Thanks to the white lies of imagination, Mirabelle liked to think about him. When she turned eleven, she decided to fall in love and chose the shepherd boy for her object. Back in Algeria after spending the summer at Sciroccu, she allowed his hair to grow out, fixed up his rotten teeth, refined his character, which was naturally gentle and brave. She made up further talents for him – riding, chestnut pastries, butterfly stroke, which only people with proper muscles can swim – and became quite convinced of the boy's qualities, even allowing him (in her daydreams, given that all of it was daydreamed) to tickle her toes with a frond of broom. Mirabelle gave him a name and described, in the most minute, improvised detail, her encounter with Dumè – she could not imagine any more Corsican name than this – to her schoolfriends in Oran. Suspicious, her girlfriends demanded a photo and they were not disappointed. The black-and-white portrait was met with sighs. Encouraged by their envious compliments, Mirabelle described the kisses that had been exchanged. The photo passed from hand to hand. Mirabelle's father Georges cut a striking figure in that portrait of 1918, in his soldier's uniform. The girls were in raptures and Mirabelle couldn't get over being the beloved of such a perfect fiancé. The deception did not spoil her pleasure. She was amazed to discover that ideas alone, mere made-up stories, could bring happiness. Their relationship had its ups and downs. One morning, the idyll took a turn towards tragedy – Dumè had written to say he loved another. But the following week, love triumphed – in a letter of repentence scented with myrtle, Dumè promised to marry his beloved Mirabelle upon his return from the war (he had become an officer). Her schoolfriends quivered with envious emotion. On the last Sunday in January, Nassim kissed Mirabelle on the summit of Aïdour, and his moist, troubling kiss killed off the shepherd, for whom Mirabelle discovered a sudden contempt. On the first day of

April, Mirabelle's father announced to his wife that he was leaving her and going to live with Ouarda. Everyone thought it was an April Fool: Ouarda, Mirabelle's nanny, was nineteen years old. Unsettled by Jeanne's screams, Georges saw fit to explain that the young Moroccan had the body of a nineteen-year-old but the soul of a centenarian, having brought up her five younger brothers and confronted material difficulties the likes of which bourgeois people like them had not the slightest comprehension. Mirabelle was twelve. A few weeks later, Violette was born, surrounded by water, on the bridge of *Ville d'Alger*, as the ship drew away from the African coast, her monumental red chimneys with their black tips rising into the storm. Jeanne scolded the student who supervised the impromptu birth – a medieval history student – for not washing his hands before officiating. Throughout the next summer, Jeanne cried constantly, while Violette, in a magical effort of compensation, did not give a single squawk. Mirabelle watched over her little sister. She felt an infinite affection for this perfect doll that docilely allowed itself to be dressed, fed, changed and bathed. Violette lavished smiles of gratitude on her sister, at which Mirabelle was perfectly delighted – and so relegated to childish pleasures the feeling of maternal joy for years inspired by her celluloid dolls. With none of the bother of waiting, growing up, finding a husband, falling pregnant, nor the pain of giving birth, Mirabelle had a child. She told Violette: 'I am your little mummy and I love you.' Violette laughed. Mirabelle pushed the pram in the streets of Marseille, chaperoned by her grandmother Joséphine, who had been born in Sciroccu, in a room with a view of goats, on the day of the Eiffel Tower's inauguration. Joséphine strolled with her pearl-grey parasol, explaining to Mirabelle that she ought to feel sorry for her mother and forgive her everything because there were three ways to lose a man – to sickness, to war and to another woman – and that of these three possibilities the last was the cruellest. Joséphine had lost her uncle, her husband and her two brothers to war. Her uncle to a cannonball in the battle of Saint-Privat on 18 August 1870, her husband by a bullet in the heart at Chemin des Dames on 16 April 1917, and both her brothers to asphyxiation a few months after their return from Verdun, in February 1917. While Mirabelle slipped spoonfuls of purée into the delighted mouth, the groans and sobs of a wounded beast could be heard. 'Don't be afraid, little Violette, it's just *maman* crying.' She reassured the baby so as to reassure herself, as all mothers do. Mirabelle had never caught her parents making love. In Oran they had slept in separate bedrooms. Jeanne rarely used to speak to Georges, and then always coldly and in an exasperated tone. She scolded him for chewing his supper with his mouth open, for letting his colleagues at the university walk all over him, for reeking of stale tobacco, for being soft with the staff and too familiar with the nanny, for spoiling Mirabelle, and for being more interested in plants than he was in human beings. Georges gave Jeanne exotic flowers, fabulous prototypes conceived in his greenhouse laboratory. 'Bring me flowers, Dodo, not monsters,' Jeanne snapped. Yet Mirabelle guessed that love can be made out even upside down, can jumble words, reverse intonations and yet be revealed in a language of paradox, in the negative, like photographic film. Jeanne loved Georges and realised it, perversely, only once she was alone and magnanimous. In Algeria, Jeanne carried her head high, wore ropes of pearls, embroidered tunics, jasmine scent, a chignon beneath a fine resin hairpin. Once in Marseille, Jeanne lived in her nightdress, skipped meals, stared at the floor rather than see Mirabelle and the baby nestled in her arms, spent her nights consulting tarot cards to confirm her bad luck, smoked for the first time in her life, luxuriated in the wreaths she breathed out, smoked non-stop, smoked, coughed and spat, smoked the same cigarettes as Georges.

Lawrence sits on the monks' bench. Mirabelle looks out through the window at the fig tree, dead of old age, that had, in times past, provided shade for her shepherd boy.

'Tell me what happened.'

'The same as usual.'

'Mira . . . Explain . . .'

'You're an egotist, Lawrence.'

'Ok . . . But now I'm here. So tell me . . . You had an argument with Baptiste . . .'

'You're an egotist and you don't see a thing. You say "tell me" . . . with that smile of yours . . . All I can reply is that everything's fine.'

'What?'

'You don't even realise. No one wants to bother you with their problems.'

'Mira, bother me with your problems.'

'Do you know what Baptiste is doing?'

'No.'

'But you do. Even though you've never said anything to me.'

'I tried . . . I said you could do with a gentler man . . . Do you remember? It was here, one summer . . .'

'A gentler man! You disembarked along with Fleur, Marine

and Justine! You were in charge! It was awful, Lawrence ... I introduced Baptiste to my family, my home ... My mother planned all our meals according to what you liked to eat ... There was no one but you ... Your passion for the hospital! Your childhood in Dublin! Your ballerina wife! Your daughters both top of their classes! Baptiste had just joined the philharmonic at the national radio network – but not one question! First cello! Baptiste was beating me and what did you say? A gentler man! You are the worst coward on the planet.'

Mirabelle knows Lawrence. She would prefer to know him less well and have something to hope for. He is going to lay his hand, gently, on her shoulder, to show his affection for her, his heroic lack of bitterness. Stumble over his words, make excuses, drop his guard – never. Get angry? Anger only surfaces through a thin skin. Swear at Mirabelle? Pure fantasy. The words would form an upside-down declaration of love, feelings made public, a backward step. Lawrence is the king of the dodge. He knows how to preserve his distance. Bodies are his business. As for feelings, this is where he's alone, by himself in his cave of craziness. He can evade anything. Intimacy; doubts; regrets. He could run through a rainstorm without getting wet. Mirabelle's heart is beating fit to burst. She feels as though it will explode and blood will spurt from her breasts like vile milk. She will fall and quiver on the ground, an unhappy fish out of water, flapping her tail on the waxed red tiles of her childhood. Lawrence will eat her for supper with a drizzle of olive oil, lemon and a bayleaf. He will invite Jeanne, Violette and all the women who're in love with him to share his supper. The table will be endless. Kilometres of drooping women, bald, exhausted, blonde, laughing like drains, ageing, still suckling at their mother's breasts, resigned, red-headed, mad, sure of themselves and deluded.

Mirabelle watches Lawrence stand up. As long as he does not leave the room without saying anything, without an embrace, taking with him only his forgiving smile. With the others, Mirabelle has some pride. With Lawrence, she has nothing. No courage; not the least little smidgen of hope. She will drop to her knees, cling to his legs, ask his pardon, say the opposite of what she said, think the opposite of what she thought. *You couldn't do anything. You tried to help me. Baptiste is a violent person. I make excuses for him. I've always been afraid of being alone. I have stayed with him so as not to be alone with myself, cut off from you.*

Lawrence puts his hand on Mirabelle's head and she feels their youth run through her body; the melted snow of winters spent waiting for someone, the blue ink of letters, beautiful letters, reread, learned and read aloud, the sticky oils of slow-moving years, the freezing wind in midsummer.

The door to the bedroom with its view over the goats closes behind Lawrence, unresisting, without a slam, as if the sounds, rich and muffled, were resonating from the depths of the bay, there, on the other side of the house, on the side where girls risk feeling too much emotion, growing up into ambitious women, into explorers, into men.

VII

From the faces raised skywards, the throats unwoolled, the buds, the tender leaves, the bare ankles on café terraces, it must be spring. Lawrence is renting an apartment, a two-bedroom place in the eaves on rue des Martyrs. Héloïse is in seventh heaven in the living room, facing directly west. In heaven in the bedroom, facing east. One day the lift stopped between the third and fourth floors. Héloïse called the lift a fascist and a dung beetle. Every second that passes is another irretrievably missed kiss. Since then, it's only the 132 threadbare, purple velvet-covered steps dropping away one by one beneath her feet. She doesn't knock and he opens the door. Her smile vanishes when she sees him. He takes her in his arms; every Friday, she leaves school, crosses Paris via its substrata, comes out at Pigalle, runs and she is there, out of breath, in a skirt, an alibi, an hour to kill. In the bathroom there is a soap dish shaped like an angel, a cloud print shower curtain, two bird-headed towel hooks and a statue of the Virgin mounted above the mirror. The previous tenant electrocuted herself in the bath.

'Of course vibrations matter . . . This apartment has excellent ones . . . I'm not making it up; my mother is from Piedmont and the Piedmontese never lie. Every man and his dog knows that . . . You can feel them straight away when you come in, can't you? Good vibes . . . True serenity . . . Besides – God keep her soul – the last tenant was smiling like a saint when they found her in the bath . . . You already knew about that, of course . . . People talk too much . . . Neighbours . . . A hairdryer, I'm sorry to say . . . an ordinary hairdryer.'

The owner of the whole building, Madame Pipistrello, is sugar sweet and assailed by nervous tics that redouble their attack when she talks about money. Eyelids powdered to midnight blue, rings set with large and dubious-looking gemstones, Suze bitters overlaid by cologne on her breath, dress worn down to the weft, voluminous and shapeless in her silk flounces, tutus and damask petticoats, threadbare, pathetic. In order to talk to you, she grips you by the wrist in just the way a buzzard sinks its claws into a fieldmouse.

'Primary residence or pied-à-terre . . . if you don't mind my asking?'

'I'm often travelling around the country due to my work, so I'm looking for a small—'

'What field do you work in, just for—'

'Medicine . . . Paediatrics . . . These days I do a lot of teaching out of town and abroa—'

'So you're not a back specialist, I suppose? My back is killing me! Look, here . . . When it hurts there when you lift your arms and then there's a pain here when you put them down . . . what does that mean, Doctor?'

'Haven't the least . . . Could it be your lumbar vertebrae?'

'My lumbar vertebrae? What a curse it is to grow old! But I can't complain; I've eyes like a hawk! I get that from my mother . . . a Piedmontese . . . All the Piedmontese have good eyes. And so, it'll just be for you then . . . your pied-à-terre?'

'My daughter will be visiting.'

'I have two daughters, myself . . . Three if you count their brother . . . Does she have work out of town? Or abroad?'

'Oh no, she's still young, she—'

'Dear God! She has lost her mother!'

'She . . . Yes. I'm still . . . Last winter.'

'It's terrible to say this, but I knew it! I can sense these things . . . Poor little mite! Don't listen to what they say: if you want my opinion, find yourself another wife as quick as you can! I don't mean to offend but . . . men don't know how to keep a house and the little girl will be wanting a mother . . . An accident, was it? Well, that's none of my business! Cancer?'

'A car accident.'

'Frightful! Frightful, frightful, frightful . . . And what's the little girl's name?'

'Héloïse.'

'How old is she?'

'Thirteen.'

'*Ooh-là!* Thirteen? No! Now, you take care! If you want my opinion, better keep an eye on that one! I hope you won't take this the wrong way but young ladies of that age are already getting ideas about things! Thirteen – she's not a little girl any more!'

'I quite agree with you, madam. I keep a close eye on her.'

'My mother used to say: a father should always watch his daughter like a jealous lover!'

'Wise words.'

'Funny you should say that . . . She spoke four languages, you know . . .'

'No . . . That's amazing . . .'

'. . . Italian, Piedmontese . . . She was from Piedmont, as I told you . . . Russian and . . . I'm forgetting one . . .'

'French?'

'French! In any case, as for the decoration, I hope you'll do as you please . . . But if you do want to change the wallpaper, please keep it classic . . . And don't do anything to the bathroom! It's gorgeous, and besides, it holds memories . . . I shan't tell you my life story but it does hold memories . . . What happened in that bathroom, well it's my business really . . .'

'Could you remind me of the rent . . . ?'

'. . . what was his name again, botheration . . .'

'Excuse me, but I see time's getting on . . .'

'Jean! Jean Fournier! Common as they come. And a good-looking man to boot! Not unlike yourself . . . a . . . You have a bit of an accent there, haven't you? You're—'

'Irish on my father's side.'

'There we are! To be quite honest, I was afraid for a second you might be German! You won't take it the wrong way, will you . . . You're not offended?'

'What? Could you just remind me of the rent . . . In your ad, I thought it seemed rather—'

'Let's see now! You're a widower . . . And there's the little girl . . . You can have a special rate!'

And all the good landlady's tics came out to play.

The cold china of the basin against her bottom. Lawrence's mouth. Héloïse clenches her teeth. He breathes on her

76

crotch, licks a part that has no name, right beside her vagina, at length. His tongue parts the lips of her sex. Something stings Héloïse: he must have done this a lot to do it so well. He has had other girls, women, lists of names, other apartments beneath other roofs that have seen it all before. The same splinter of despair pricks Lawrence: *Nothing lasts, she will leave, I'll make her leave, time will destroy us as it has destroyed all the others.*

'You know what I really like?'

'Tell me, my little lion.'

'When you spit. Don't you remember?'

'No.'

'On the edge of the sink . . . I had my legs round your waist . . .'

'Vaguely . . .'

'Stop it! You were going very fast . . . Like that . . . You were pushing right to the end of my pussy . . .'

'Héloïse! "My pussy"! Since when . . . At your age, I thought pussy meant the cat's wife.'

'When you were my age, it was the Middle Ages. Are you listening or not?'

'I'm trying . . .'

'You were pushing your cock fast into my pussy . . . You stopped . . . and you spat in my mouth.'

'Perhaps I like you so much that you make me do all kinds of crazy things.'

'No! It's just I like it when you do dirty stuff.'

'Don't say that.'

'I loved you then, suddenly, when you spat.'

'Didn't you love me before, Scarlett?'

'Rhett, I did love you . . . but just then, I really believed in it . . . I want to die, sometimes, I love you so much.'

'You *are* romantic, my little lion . . .'

'You're always teasing me.'

'No, I worship you.'

'Will you spit in my mouth again?'

'No.'

'Will you slap me?'

'Calm down.'

'We could be on a beach . . . No! In the jungle in Burma . . . No, wait! On a cruise ship! OK? In the middle of the Pacific . . . in a cabin . . . with just one guy who's looking at us, a sailor with tattoos of bears on his arms, and I'll be . . .'

'Lose the sailor.'

'. . . sitting on you . . . completely naked . . . with my nipples really hard . . . Can you picture it?'

'Not really.'

'Yes you can. As if I was going to pee . . . You would watch me go up and down . . . like this . . . and this . . . You'll be so, so, so, so excited . . .'

'I get seasick on boats.'

'. . . and then you would give me a slap! Thwack!'

'Héloïse . . .'

'Say you would.'

'I wouldn't.'

'Then tell me you would do dirty things to me.'

'No, you're too pretty.'

'Lawrence, stop! You're treating me like a child!'

'Never.'

'You are. You think I'm too young. Am I too young for you?'

'I think you're very lucky to be so young.'

'You see! You think I'm too young!'

'No, you're perfectly young . . . perfect . . . You are a miracle, Héloïse! I'm mad about you.'

'What about my slap?'

VIII

An arrogant creature lives in Barnabé's stomach. A wading bird with sublime plumage and a vicious beak that gouges at the flesh of his belly button. Héloïse is torture. Barnabé follows her every Friday as she hurries to leave school. Keeping to the same side of the road as Héloïse, he stays hidden, hunched, a bare outline only a few metres behind her adored skirts that change colour, cut, season, worn with or without tights, and the three long strings of beads bouncing on her breasts, her joyful legs, her shoes soaking up rain, frost, hot paving stones, the heels she puts on at the corner of the street, always perching on the same bench. She stuffs the other pair into her bag. Flat school shoes exchanged for scorpion-sting heels. Poisonous shoes. Barnabé is sure they are a present. He finds them vulgar: too high, too red, too contorted. They turn Héloïse into someone else, someone older, with a different walk. Héloïse is ugly in her big tart's heels and she's going to trip. She doesn't trip. She is beautiful. Her grace is unimpaired. The shoes are sculpted for her slender feet. Other people are also looking at her. Barnabé is not alone, stalking her butterfly zigzags. Everyone sees her. She hooks in men of all ages on the pavements, in cars, in cafés: wasps clustering around her beauty. Before stepping inside the building, she looks right and left several times; she is flying as high as the tiny puff of cloud above – what a thrill to have to keep this secret. Behind Héloïse: Barnabé. Inside the building. A twilit entrance hall, letter boxes with oblong grins, a ray of sunlight, dust dancing, Héloïse's back, Barnabé, breathing in gasps, temples pounding, a thread of sweat in his hair, and then the sound of keys. Héloïse is going to see a boy who has given her keys. Therefore he is not a boy, he is a man. No parents, no rules or study. Worse: a profession, a salary, a car, a bed twice as wide as Barnabé's. Coffee, cigarettes, wine, routines, the fabulous world of adults. Twenty-five, perhaps thirty years old. He'll have to fight the years to catch up. They're in love. They're lovers. He knows how to do everything. Kisses, touches, fingers, lips. Those mysterious configurations – the 'positions'. They do positions. He knows every one of her smells: her armpits, hair, saliva, feet, the juice she makes. She knows all his smells, bitter, smoky. Barnabé wants to die. Héloïse must take him for just an irritating kid. The more Fridays he follows her traitress heels, his teeth gritted, the more precisely he hates himself, body part by body part, his voice, his tears always about to well over. Barnabé needs all this pain that Héloïse causes him. With some imagination, it is love. His appetite aroused, the struggle between joy and despair, embraces and bites thrown together. The darkness in the hallway is so different from that of the cupboard they shared when they were small. The hearts in the biscuit tin, mouths sticky with kisses and apricot jam. Héloïse unzips her rucksack and rummages. Barnabé would like to watch her undress, undo her hair and tell herself whatever people say at moments like this. The imagination is crueller than the plain, raw truth.

To get inside Héloïse's head, to know her thoughts. A packet. She's bought something at the bakery. A nice thought. A little gesture. The packet bobs at the end of a string. Barnabé has already tried to kiss her. In front of the school gates, head tipped to one side; in Héloïse's eyes a humid gleam that was impossible to interpret, that Barnabé had finally taken for encouragement. He had leant towards her, she, as if squashing a fly, had crushed his mouth with her finger. Not once in his detailed daydreams, these scenarios replayed a hundred times, had Barnabé imagined that Héloïse would reject his lips and all his courage with one hand. Héloïse had sighed. Barnabé had followed her down the street. Side by side, underground, they had descended the staircases and commented on a poster ad. Never had the clinical tiles of the metro's corridors seemed more strange to Barnabé – an illogical and infinite bathroom that never led to a bath, like in those nightmares in which people swap faces and reverse roles without ever rousing the dreamer's suspicions. Barnabé and Héloïse had sat on two folding seats next to each other and described how they would spend their millions if they won the lottery. Not a word, in the metro or ever after, about the attempted kiss.

Héloïse stops in front of the mirror and tidies her hair with her fingers. The packet dangles at the end of the string. Perhaps a coffee eclair. An opera cake. A black forest gateau. Some sweet pastry adored by his rival. Barnabé is about to hear his voice: deep, obviously. Nothing. Only the slam of a door. A discreet slam, practised, repeated a thousand times. Barnabé stays there by the letter boxes for a long time, reading the names. BERNARDI. MAURET. EL-FASSI. ROUSSEAU-ELOI.

PEVERGNE. DE BUSSCHER. CHABBI. SARL. LEXANE. THOMAS. MANKOUR. THONNEAU. AKRIRE. PHUTHAKHAN. GAZQUEZ. LECOMTE. Outside these walls, do they hold hands? Does he call her Héloïse? My darling? My angel? My busy bee? Or some other nickname, idiotic to everyone else but perfectly sweet and serious for people who are in love. Barnabé has anticipated making threats. *This is the last time I'll be your alibi on Friday. I'll tell your mother everything. I'll tell her where you go and what you do.* The threats stayed put, going nowhere, in his head. Barnabé does everything secretly – love letters, floods of tears, hiccoughs, a melancholy wank. No regrets: Héloïse would have found some other alibi for her Fridays. Barnabé hears his breathing, as if they were both there together in the hallway: little Barnabé and the grown-up one. He sees the minuscule dust particles dancing in the single ray of sun and thinks to himself: *That's God*, just to be silly, although it does make him look up. He thinks again of the messed-up kiss and of Héloïse's sigh right afterwards. In that sigh, Barnabé decided, there had been something of their childhood, a note of regret for when they were slave-traders; surgeons amputating limbs at Verdun; pirates shipwrecked on the Sandwich Islands; Carmelite nuns being whipped by their mother superior; zealots rowing in the lowest deck of a Spanish galleon; survivors of a rocket crash marooned on Jupiter; orphans running away from their austere institution so as to escape Monsieur and Madame Horribilus, come to adopt them; highwaymen knocking marchionesses about and relieving them of their gold-lined undergarments; prisoners in Alcatraz reduced to eating flat-tened rats beneath the ironing board – that is, to eating slices of buttered toast with grated chocolate left at their feet by

Mirabelle, in the spirit of the game – 'Here, assassins, is your meagre share: stale bread and water.' Sometimes she would play it even better: 'Chew it well, you foul vermin, for 'tis your last meal in this world; in one hour you will be sent to hang by your necks until you be dead.' The expression made Héloïse shiver with pleasure. *Hang . . . 'til you be dead.* She would swoon in the arms of her companion in misfortune.

Barnabé is not too sad. Héloïse is up there, in someone's arms, but she can have only one soulmate forged in the womb of their childhood. Never again will she feel a joy as pure as sharing their last earthly slices of toast as men condemned to the gallows. Never again such strange excitement as when using a wet dishcloth to whip the naked buttocks of Barnabé, her rebellious Carmelite. This sanctuary that each person guards in their eternal memory of the other is the sweetest of consolations. Barnabé is the image and the voice of those first years; Héloïse, ever his childish fiancée.

IX

The beach. Saturday.

'Look what I've found on my tummy . . .'
　'You'll catch a cold.'
　'Had you seen this one before?'
　'Yes. Put your clothes back on.'
　'. . . it's grown, it's a new one . . .'
　'You've always had it and you have another one the same on your groin.'
　'My what?'
　'Groin. That's your groin, there.'
　'Do you know all my beauty spots?'
　'On first-name terms with 'em.'
　'But truly . . . can you remember where they all are, with your eyes closed?'
　'Not one spot of beauty may escape my wisdom. Alexandrine.'
　'What?'
　'Twelve syllables.'
　'Stop. You'd think you were Madame Falakros . . .'
　'Which one is she, now? French?'
　'I've told you a hundred times.'

'I know, but you have to tell me things lots of times if you want them to stick in my old head.'

'No, it's just that you don't listen. Oh what is it we can see now? Is it England?'

'It's a dog, my sweet. A spaniel.'

'Over there, Lawrence! Straight ahead! It's the English coast! It's your home!'

'I'm Irish, Héloïse.'

'Same thing! That grey bit – it's London!'

'London! My little Scarlett . . . We haven't a hope of seeing London from the beaches of Normandy. I shall buy you a map of Europe . . .'

'I'd rather have a wedding dress.'

'That Madame Falakros, what does she teach you, again?'

'French.'

'That's what I said.'

'You're so annoying.'

'I'm going to arrange private tuition for you, otherwise you'll have to retake the year.'

'You'll be wasting your money. I'm always going off on tangents at school.'

'And why is that, my darling little rebel?'

'Other ideas come into my head.'

'And what tangent have you chosen for your latest essay?'

'Dissertation.'

'Dissertation then, sweetheart.'

'I wrote about you.'

'Me? Lawrence Calvagh?'

'Under a code name! I called you my one true love, who's forty years older than me.'

'That's fiendishly well coded, Scarlett.'

'Why, thank you, Rhett.'

'Do you want my jacket?'

'No.'

'What was it actually about?'

'A boring question on Sophocles's *Antigone* and Anouilh's *Antigone* . . . "*By sacrificing herself for the sake of love and justice, Antigone turns herself into an unintelligent small-time crystal-gazer who ultimately does not understand the cause that she is dying for. Comment on this statement, justifying your response . . .*"'

'But that's you all over – Antigone! Stubborn as mules, the both of you! Queens of disobedience and transgression!'

'What does that make you?'

'I am the doctor, madam. How is our little Héloïse this morning?'

'Not well. She's lost her appetite. She doesn't care about anything . . . She's getting terrible marks . . . Always daydreaming . . . I'm afraid she may have caught the disease . . .'

'What disease, madam?'

'The disease of love!'

'In that case, madam, we must give up hope! Medicine can do nothing for your child!'

'Save her, Doctor! I beseech you!'

'I prefer to lead her to her ruin.'

'Excuse me, Doctor?'

'I am a satyr . . . I eat young Héloïses for breakfast every day . . . A wolf in doctor's clothing . . .'

'Have you always wanted to be a doctor, my love?'

'Absolutely not. I wanted to be an opera singer.'

'Lawrence . . .'

'I'm serious! I was in my college choir in Dublin. And I did seven years at the Paris Conservatoire. I had a very fine voice, I'll have you know. A bass that would have you quaking on the spot.'

'I love your voice.'

'It is literally extraordinary.'

'You are funny . . .'

'Yes, I'm hilarious.'

'How shall we put it . . . A dry wit?'

'I don't know what you're talking about, Scarlett. And those flippers look ravishing on you.'

'These are not flippers, Rhett, these are the stilettos that you bought me to mark three years of our love.'

'You are right to wear them on the wet sand, they only cost me two thousand two hundred francs.'

'Two thousand two hundred francs!'

'I love you, Scarlett, what can I do . . . ?'

'I want you to tell me that you will be my love until I die.'

'Your loyal servant fears he may not survive to see that tragic day.'

'Stop it! People live to a hundred! Olive oil! People who drink lots of olive oil live to a hundred and ten!'

'I shall touch no other beverage, my beloved.'

'Lawrence?'

'Yes, Mademoiselle Herschel?'

'What did you sing when you used to sing?'

'Goodness . . . Dr Bartolo in *The Marriage of Figaro*. . . the doctor in *Pelléas et Mélisande*. . . the high priest Sarastro in *The Magic Flute* . . .'

'Really? I can't tell if you're teasing me . . .'

'Of course I'm not, darling lion!'

'You never talk about it.'

'I'm a private young man.'

'Sing me some opera.'

'Now?'

'Sing me your bit from *Figaro*.'

'For the benefit of this seagull?'

'Oh, it's only got one foot!'

'Poor creature.'

'It must feel left out . . . Look, the others have left it by itself . . . The rest are all together in the flock . . .'

'We ought to take it back to the hotel, then in Paris I could make it a prosthetic claw.'

'Could you really do that?'

'No.'

'But would it be possible, medically speaking?'

'A prosthetic seagull's foot?'

'Can it be done?'

'Are you teasing me?'

'We could at least take it back to the hotel and give it something to eat . . .'

'Scarlett, let's stop making a spectacle of ourselves . . . The police are already waiting for us in the hotel lobby . . .'

'You're paranoid . . .'

'That guy's face at reception when I asked for the room! He knew what was going on!'

'Not at all . . . He thought you were my grandfather.'

'You're an angel, Héloïse.'

'You prefer him to think I'm your sixteen-year-old tart?'

'You have the same voice as your mother . . .'

'Excuse me, I'm—'

'Precisely the same inflection . . .'

'Are you angry with me?'

'. . . a kind of caustic hissing in the high notes.'

'Fine, you're angry with me.'

'I was with your mother thirty-five years ago. Do you ever think about that?'

'You have an idea you're in love with the same woman only grown young again . . . And perhaps you'll also fall in love with my daughter and my daughter's daughter . . . So you'll love us all without stopping and love will make you immortal.'

'You are joyous and tragic in the space of a second . . . Your mother was unhappy . . . I made her unhappier still.'

'Young love is always unhappy . . .'

'Says my lion with the wisdom of her sixteen years!'

'And a half.'

'At what age do you stop counting the halves . . .'

'Who left who? You or *maman*?'

'We had a kind of accident.'

'Both of you?'

'Mirabelle became pregnant – by me.'

'What? You had a baby?'

'I was twenty-one . . . Mirabelle was so fragile . . .'

'What did you do? Did you give it away?'

'Héloïse . . . No . . . There was never a baby . . . Mirabelle began to bleed at the end of the third month . . . She miscarried . . . and I was . . .'

'Relieved?'

'No, not relieved.'

'Come on. Let's go back to the hotel.'

The hotel bedroom. Sunday.

'Shall we go for a swim?'

'Obviously, as the sea is thirteen degrees today. What are you reading?'

'*The Hunting of the Snark.*'

'Fantastic! Lewis Carroll . . . Is it for school?'

'I am capable of choosing a book for myself.'

'I didn't mean . . . Are you enjoying it?'

'Yes . . . I don't understand a word.'

'It's very poetic . . . completely absurd . . .'

'*Car le Snark, bel et bien, était un Boujoum, figurez-vous!*'*

'Héloïse! You must read it in English! It's a poem! You have to hear the words in English!'

'Here, then . . . Read it to me in your voice. Start here.'

> '"*Just the place for a Snark!*" *the Bellman cried,*
> *As he landed his crew with care;*
> *Supporting each man on the top of the tide*
> *By a finger entwined in his hair . . .*'

'No! First fuck me in the bath and then you can read the *Snark* to me!'

---

* 'For, although common Snarks do no manner of harm,
   Yet, I feel it my duty to say,
Some are Boojums—'
– Lewis Caroll

'Your wish is my command, Mademoiselle Herschel.'

'You want to know what I'm thinking?'

'Tell me.'

'No, I meant . . . are you interested in what is going through my mind? Do you want to know why I'm here with you?'

'I make the most of every second before you vanish, my dragonfly.'

'But we're going to spend our whole lives together!'

'Our lives . . . I'm fifty-six . . . And you have an eyelash . . .'

'Don't touch; I'm making a wish.'

'Have you made it?'

'Wait! It's the most important wish of my life . . .'

'My God.'

'There, you can take it now. Shall I tell you my wish?'

'Heavens, no.'

'Why not?'

'Because even if you're 100 per cent convinced to the contrary, one day you are going to meet someone . . . you'll want to have children . . .'

'I already want to have children.'

'You see.'

'With you.'

'That will never happen, Héloïse. It's unthinkable.'

'Why?'

'At my age . . . Héloïse, I already have children and they're adults now.'

'They're not children any more if they're adults.'

'My dear lion, what I'm trying to tell you is that the time is past . . . Justine used to ride her tricycle in the hallway of our apartment and now she is going to have her photos in one of the biggest galleries in New York . . . You can't imagine how time passes . . . Marine has three children! Her eldest, Caroline, and the twins . . . you met them last summer in Corsica . . . Maxime and Benjamin . . .'

'What's this got to do with our baby?'

'A baby? I'm a grandfather three times over! You have no idea, Héloïse . . . Marine often leaves the twins with us at the weekend and Fleur is in seventh heaven, but me . . . The shattered nights . . . the crying . . . going off to bore myself shitless in some park . . . yoghurt in my hair . . . the tantrums . . . Your tantrums were . . . You were a superb baby . . . You were dazzling . . .'

'We won't have a child?'

'You will have your own children.'

'I hate you.'

'Héloïse! Even if we had a baby on the day you turn eighteen . . .'

'Oh yes! On my eighteenth birthday! We can call him Krishna!'

'Krishna? Can't you choose a proper name . . .'

'You can call him whatever you like, but I shall call him Krishna.'

'I shall be eighty years old when Krishna is twenty!'

'But at twenty, you don't need a father any more! Even before then—'

'My lion, you don't seem to need anyone . . . but eighty years old! You will be madly beautiful and I . . . Eighty . . .'

'Age doesn't mean a thing.'

'You'll change your mind . . . I shan't be able to get it up any more . . . I'll have lost the last of my teeth . . .'

'Won't you still have a tongue?'

'If I'm lucky.'

'Then you shall lick out my pussy twenty times a day so as to make me come twenty times a day.'

'My Héloïse . . .'

'And you will be handsome when you're eighty! You'll hardly look seventy.'

'A young man.'

'A handsome young Englishman.'

'Irish.'

'Same thing.'

X

In Brooklyn, in a former foundry, the fuschia-painted anvils now serve as low stools. The fireplace, a great gleaming maw, holds plastic cups and petits fours in serried tiers. Five-metre-high stained glass windows, narrow as arrow slits, rose from the floor to split the whitewashed walls. The exhibition is called NAILS and the invitation to the private view reads:

Justine Calvagh was born in 1966. Her father was a doctor and her mother a ballet dancer. Fingernails have been her passion from an early age. She spent ten years varnishing thousands of nails, then a further ten years criss-crossing the globe, taking photographs of thousands more nails.

In the *Big Apple Art Review*, art critic Emily Wig wrote:

Justine Calvagh's outsize formats reveal the human touch via our extremities. Apparently extraneous and impervious to pain, nails encapsulate the idyll of the vast and the tiny.

In the widely read *American Art Gossip*, Isabel Blickstein wrote:

In Paris, India, London, New Zealand, China, Japan, Morocco, Peru, New York and on an island off the coast of Turkey, Justine Calvagh has pursued an enterprise at once titanic and antlike: that of photographing all the fingernails of humankind.

In *Crazy Pygmalion*, which devoted a five-page special to Justine's work, Graham Pennington wrote:

Clean, filthy, embellished, disfigured, Calvagh's nails are open books. The twisted nail of a Hindu sadhu, the moribund nails of a junkie in Queens, the stuck-on false nails of a London prostitute, the nails bitten down to the quick of a New York trader: all these massively magnified fingernails speak of opulence, vice, slums, magical rites, tough jobs, velvet gloves, youth and old age, flirtation, sickness and hale good health.

In the very underground *Eat & Fuck*, Maxie Holsen wrote:

The more in-yer-face the better. When dyke Justine Calvagh has nothing left to say, she screams at us. Great oversized things clearly get her nice and wet. Perhaps a reminder of her distant hetero past. But even at two metres by three, her photos bug me. You won't believe it but the other evening, I rock up at my friend's place – Betty Lost's, the legendary guitarist of the group Funny Paedophile – and what do I see in her john? A nail by the great artist! You reply: 'A nail by Justine Calvagh?! Betty's bog must be a palace!' And so it is! The thing is, she's rich, the silly bitch! Her last album, Crustaceans, a pure masterpiece of rococo-garage-rock, sold 400,000 copies. Betty doesn't even need her producer Greg Teuer any more, to finance the kilos of coke she hoovers up

her nose! And now she can take a piss while admiring a $50,000
nail that she can't even use to scratch her ass. In short, if you
enjoy yawning and puking, it's all going on at the Shark Gallery,
Church Avenue, Brooklyn.

The Shark Gallery is packed out. Fragments of conversations burble across each other. Héloïse looks for Lawrence in the crowd of guests. The Garett sisters appear, hug her, whisper into her neck, congratulate her in their high, honking voices. They say that Pete Irving is planning to buy *Famille III* ('Family III'). Héloïse elbows her way through the painted mouths and the unsteady glasses, brimful of champagne. The ash of cigarettes furiously and continually smoked is snowing down onto the cement slabs of the floor. Héloïse overhears comments, dirty rag-ends of them. 'Justine's problem is her own success.' Héloïse thinks she spots Lawrence but it isn't him, it doesn't even look like him. 'She does the same photos over and over, she's so afraid of fucking up.' Héloïse has not spoken to Lawrence for six months. She failed her Baccalaureate. He said that she wouldn't get anywhere without her Bac, that France is full of idiots with qualifications. She shrugged. He took her arms and shook her. She gave him a scratch on his Adam's apple. They didn't see each other for twenty-seven days. Lawrence spent 190,000 francs at the Drouot auction house. He fainted in a supermarket aisle. He wept on Fleur's shoulder. He waited for Héloïse in the rue des Martyrs apartment. He called her place. He hung up – it was Mirabelle who answered. He followed Héloïse in the street. She called for help. People stopped in the street. Lawrence retreated back home.

Héloïse knocks into a tall obese girl. Pretzels go flying. Héloïse crouches to pick them up. 'Up you get, poppet! The less I pig out, the less goes on my butt!' Héloïse gazes at a two-metre-high fingernail, yellowed by tobacco, and the words LUCKY DAYS in wide letters on the white-ish half-moon. 'In any case, now that Justine's worth what she's worth, there's more than one critic ready to take a hatchet to her work.' Héloïse stops in the small last room of the exhibition, where her own photographs are on display. *Héloïse Herschel, born in 1977 in Ajaccio.* Five photos at once related and unfamiliar. When Justine showed them to the director of the Shark Gallery, he had said: 'I'm shocked,' hand flat to his forehead, pitch-perfect drama queen, even though he always meant what he said. He had bought *Famille II* ('Family II') for a thousand dollars. Héloïse's first sale. He had decided to show a selection of her photos at the end of the *NAILS* show, as a foretaste of a more ambitious unveiling. There are three guests examining *Thanksgiving Meal* with unreadable expressions of concentration. They leave the room. They have said nothing. But the skinny little guy with the ridiculously large red-framed glasses turns back, points to the photo and says: 'In that one, you're really somewhere else.' Héloïse doesn't know if it's a compliment or the opposite.

After twenty-seven days she called Lawrence, who didn't say a word about her ringing the forbidden telephone on Fleur's bedside table. Héloïse said she'd like to live in New York. Lawrence promised to pay her airfare and that he would take care of everything. She would live in Brooklyn with Justine, who would look after her like a little sister. He would send her money every month. Before her departure, Héloïse agreed to meet him at the apartment on rue des Martyrs. Lawrence took the stairs at a run. She wanted him to slap her softly he slapped her she wanted him to slap her without seeming to he slapped her rather sickened she wanted him to say I love you he said I love you she wanted him to have anal sex with her they had anal sex she shouted at him because he hurt her he said sorry she wanted him to sing the aria he had sung in Normandy he sang it badly she asked him to try harder he said he hadn't slept for days and days she said she would leave him if he didn't sing it he sang she wanted him to shave her pubic hair off he shaved even the delicate lips between her thighs with a trembling disposable razor she wanted him to piss on her he couldn't do it he had such an erection she begged him he got angry he called her a tyrannical little bitch he lost his erection he pulled her long honey-coloured whisky-coloured buttered-corn hair he pissed on her mouth he said she was making him crazy she said she loved him to death she asked him to come deep inside her he refused she screamed that she wanted a baby she beat her fists on the parquet floor he cried like the baby she was hoping for.

It's impossible to penetrate any further into the clamour of the Shark Gallery. The guests are hot, they're fanning themselves with their invitations. Héloïse catches the eye of Justine, queen of the evening, encircled by eight bodies that could, any second, suck her up, digest her and regurgitate her in a corner without anyone seeing a thing. Near Justine, her sister Marine is standing, thin-lipped. Her glass of apple juice is heavy in her hand. Her three children are staying in Paris with their grandmother, Fleur. Marine has forgotten to put the twins' vitamins in their washbag. She hopes Fleur will think of buying more and that she will make the children wash their hands before every meal so they don't lose their good habits. Hygiene and good habits: these things are important. Marine would like to lock herself in the loo, sit down on a toilet seat lid and take off the pearl necklace and the new shoes that are hurting her. And re-emerge at two in the morning when the guests have all left. She surveys the checked surf shorts, the slashed jeans, the skeletal model and her Alice band edged with white fur rabbits' ears. She swallows. Nothing in common with these people. Her dress and her jacket with its mother-of-pearl buttons. She pretends not to see Héloïse waving energetically to her from the other end of the room. Marine hated Héloïse's photos. She felt ignorant, humiliated, provincial. She said to herself: Héloïse is a child of the metropolis. She felt a great surge of anger in front of *Famille III*: a family of white people, father, mother, their three children, are posing in front of their bourgeois suburban house. Snow covers the lawn. They are smiling, they have put on their best spring clothes, except for the father, who is naked. The colours are dazzling and false. The blue sky is blood red. The neat little house is black all over, walls, roof, windows, the living-room bay window. The five faces are daubed with cooking oil. Their blonde hair glitters like rhinestones under the spotlights. The mother is missing an arm. The empty sleeve of her blouse flutters in the wind. Their eyes sparkle with a virtually ecstatic joy. The father, naked and skinny apart from his beer belly, has an erection. His little daughter's ear, with its gold earring, brushes his glans. The little girl is clutching a Smith & Wesson .44 magnum revolver to her chest. Tattooed on her cheek is a five-pointed blue star, emblem of the Dallas Cowboys, five-time winners of the Super Bowl. The mother's sole arm plunges into the collar of her eldest son, a black albino with widely dilated red pupils and pink irises. In front of the rest, the baby sits in a saucepan along with a Thanksgiving turkey. Héloïse waves again, trying to catch her attention, and Marine looks down. Kelly Morgan and her brother come up to Héloïse, their smiles crammed with big, ruddy gums and chemically whitened teeth, perfectly straight, mini-shelves of white books. Kelly has bought *Chien de famille* ('Family Dog'). Héloïse thanks her.

'Do you know where you'll hang it?'

'Right where I can see it! In my office at Cantor Fitzgerald, above the sofa. They'll go together perfectly!'

'What will?'

'The dog and my sofa! The sofa has the same beige tones!'

Héloïse did not feel lost when she came to New York. She missed Lawrence and, at the end of the summer, she met Hozumi. Before Héloïse's departure, Lawrence had been calling Justine whenever Fleur asked him to. He began to call her every day and sometimes twice a day. Justine talked about the technical challenges of her photos' magnification process, about the finer points involved in organising her future exhibitions at the Shark Gallery, about the artists she was meeting at her trendy parties. She reported, not omitting a single witticism, the crazy arguments she kept up with her lover Maxie Holsen, the journalist at *Eat & Fuck*. She explained why she was simultaneously head over heels and repelled. Maxie is a nutter. She sleeps with a dead chicken, a raw one with white skin straight out of the butcher's, its head cut off, which stinks of warm meat in the middle of the night. Justine rambled on for hours, touched that, for the first time in her life, her father was listening to her tales of this and that. Sometimes she talked to him about Héloïse. 'I've been lending her my cameras. She gets these strays with real loony expressions to pose for her. She finds them in the streets. She shows them what to do with just her hands; without a word of English, she gets them to take their clothes off. She's mad, that girl.' The news of Héloïse made Lawrence's heart race. The rest was a bore and an ordeal. One morning, without giving any further detail, Justine told her father that Héloïse had a boyfriend. She used the English word – *boyfriend.* Lawrence quivered; he could see his hand shaking. He enquired, heartily, after the name of this 'gentleman with such good taste'. Lawrence instantly found he hated the name Hozumi and everything Japanese. He took down the fifteenth-century Muromachi painting he had bought in Tokyo with Violette.

Héloïse hesitates before the buffet. In her mouth, crisps mingle with peanut-butter-filled chocolates. Confused tastes saturated with noxious flavourings. Her hunger grows with every mastication. Leaning over the table, the pretzel girl fills her paper plate with cubes of cheddar. She smiles at Héloïse: 'I used to spend my days eating! I'd get up in the middle of the night and empty the cupboards! Once I went out in the street in my slippers at three in the morning to get a kebab!' Héloïse notices that the woman is sweating around the mouth; it opens to bite into the gleaming puffed crust of a liver pâté canapé. Hozumi kisses Héloïse on the nose. The obese woman can't stop herself from looking, turning away and then looking again, as one looks at a handicapped body, looking away and then back again.

'Where are your photos, baby?'

'At the back, in the last room.'

'They're hiding you away! They're afraid you'll put Little

Miss Nails in the shade . . . It's so lousy what she does. Nails . . .
If it were people's stomachs, now . . . Close-ups of bellies
would be amazing.'

'How would you photograph a belly?'

'You're uptight.'

'I'm hungry.'

'You're not feeling too frazzled?'

'I'm sick of answering that question. What's in your glass?
Champagne?'

'White wine . . . it's gross. I bumped into Kelly . . . She
came with her brother . . .'

'I know. She bought *Chien de famille*.'

'Kelly? She bought the Labrador?'

'She said the dog's coat would go with the sofa in her office.'

'She's such a silly cow!'

'And the Garrett twins told me that Pete Erving wants to
buy *Famille III*.'

'Pete's told me twenty times that he'd buy one of my photos
and he never has . . . Don't get your hopes up . . . Jeez, it's
stacked with journalists in here!'

'Where?'

'The whole place! See, over there, that little skinny guy . . .'

'With the big red glasses?'

'That's Adam Atalleph.'

'Is he well known?'

'Well known? He calls the shots round here.'

'He hated my photos.'

'Did he see them?'

'He said they were a heap of crap.'

'He said that?'

'He didn't say it like that, but it comes to the same thing.'

'Although he loved my series of Polaroids on fast food trashcans. He almost wrote an article on it.'

'They were beautiful.'

'They were inspired.'

Hozumi has a face tattooed on his face. An eye beneath each eye, a mouth under his mouth, a nose below his nose. The tattoo – the face of a young girl – will never grow old. One slim cigarette, a Vogue, with its artificial bluish smoke, between the artificial red-lined lips. Beneath Hozumi's eyes, blue eyes accentuated by sparkly lashes. And narrow hazel eyebrows reaching to the flat, immobile eyelids. Two delicate faces. A monstrous marriage. One morning, Héloïse had awoken under the table in an unfamiliar kitchen. In the bedroom, the midday sun filtered through the blinds and zebraed across Hozumi's naked body. She had watched him sleep for a moment. The preceding night was vague, but Héloïse's clothes mingled with Hozumi's on the fake bearskin rug. Two voluptuous breasts were tattooed on her new lover's smooth torso. A purple vulva on his waxed thigh. A pair of skimpy, red lace knickers, rucked down, tattooed on his knees. Waking to see Héloïse standing at the foot of his bed, Hozumi had covered his breasts and his woman's genitals. With every smile, only one of his two mouths obeys his delight. The other, slightly misshapen one, twists into an inhuman expression. When Héloïse kisses the fake red mouth, her own vulva moistens with pleasure.

Lawrence is met by the anorexic model wearing canary-yellow wellies and long rabbit ears. She is drunk. Lawrence helps her sit down on a fuchsia anvil. She wraps herself around him and draws him in against her hollow-boned body.

'They used to have a forge here, you know . . .'

'So it seems. My dear, I'm exhausted, I've come straight from the airport . . . I'm here to see my daughter.'

'Will you sit on my lap?'

'Not tonight.'

'Your daughter isn't Justine?'

'You know Justine?'

'Mr Calvagh! Hell! The spit of Justine! The very spit of her!'

'Do you know her well?'

'I'm Maxie Holsen . . . She's never talked about me?'

'Maxie . . . You sleep with a chicken.'

'And I have fits of yawns when I come!'

'Justine omitted to mention that to me . . .'

'Do you like her photos? Between you and me? Honestly?'

'I find them stunning.'

'My ass! You wanna see something really stunning? Go right to the end of the gallery. Héloïse Herschel's photos . . . That's art will give you something for the wank bank!'

'What was the name you said?'

'Héloïse Herschel. A little French eighteen-year-old . . . She was squatting at your daughter's place but I think she's moved in with a Jap now . . . Boy is she cute! I'd give ten years of my life to eat her out!'

'Is she here this evening?'

'Can't miss her . . .'

'Why not?'

'How can I put it . . . ? She's filled out nicely: she's got a bun in the oven!'

107

XI

'Koko, if you bite one more jogger, I'm taking you home!'
Krishna rolls his eyes and sticks out his tongue. Springtime
fills his mouth. His wheelie crocodile rattles along behind him.
On the baseball pitch, a batter freezes, buttocks clenched,
pitched backwards, jaw square. The bat slices through the air,
misses the ball, which brushes the aromatic, saturated, freshly
cut grass and, in slow motion, scores against Koko's tail.
Krishna clutches the white leather prize with its brown
stitching. The big shadow approaches. 'Thanks dude!' Smell
of sour sweat. The ball vanishes in the big man's hand. Krishna
kneels down to ask Koko if he would like to go for a swim in
the lake. He strokes the emerald-painted wooden scales and
waggles a warning finger at him. 'As long as you don't attack
a silver heron like last time!' Krishna talks to Koko in French.
(Koko is a French-speaking crocodile, made in China, bought
in Paris by Granny Mirabelle.) A jogger goes by. Pink Lycra
sweatbands round her forehead and wrists. Great strides in
white socks. Smell of cheese. Edible calves, waxed, shining, as
if wrapped in clingfilm. Krishna observes Koko. 'If you attack
her . . .' The jogger recedes. Krishna takes a gulp of Coca-Cola
from his Spiderman flask.

'Mummy! Koko's thirsty! Can we go to the lake?'

'I promised *papa* that we'd be home by noon.'

'Please!'

'Come on Krishna . . . We'll give Koko water from the bathroom . . .'

'It's not the same! He needs water from the lake!'

'The lake is polluted, my darling . . . Tap water is better for him.'

'I already told him he could!'

'Tell him we'll go there in the afternoon.'

'He wants to go now.'

'Krishna . . . Don't start . . .'

'He'll get a dedrytation.'

'Dehydration. Come on now!'

'No. I'm staying with Koko.'

'Krishna, I'm losing my temper! Don't go and lie on the ground now!'

'But tap water is for people!'

'Do you want me to call *papa* and tell him you're having a tantrum?'

'But you promised!'

'I never promised that we'd go to the lake! I said yes to taking Koko for a walk but I never said anything about the lake.'

'You're making me sad. I think I'm going to cry.'

'Oh Krishna . . . please . . .'

'Not for a long time!'

'You're such a pain, Krishna! A real pain in the backside, dammit!'

'You're swearing.'

'Yes, I'm swearing! *Tu me casses les couilles!* You're a pain in the ass! Come on then – we're going to the lake. So you can stop being such a pain!'

'Thanks, Mum! I love you, I love you, I love you!'
Krishna hugs Héloïse's knees with grateful arms. She ruffles a finger through his hair, over his sweet, cool little cheeks. The breeze brings a scent of seawater and lilies.

Héloïse watches Krishna go cautiously up to the edge and dip Koko's head into the muddy waters of the Turtle Pond. Lawrence is waiting for them at home, doubtless sitting in the big armchair. Or standing by the sash window, so he can see the cherry blossom. It is midday. The sun. The blossoms' fairy schemes. Lawrence would have stopped Krishna from leaning so far over. Héloïse calls to him to take care. Koko laps up big mouthfuls. He re-emerges. A few springs earlier, Lawrence had left Fleur. From across the Atlantic, by telephone. Only that cowardly, courageous voice. Fleur had been unable to stop laughing, in their spacious rue de Rivoli apartment, all emptiness and echoes. She had leant on the black marble mantelpiece. The acanthus leaf-framed mirror with its marks of age and death. 'Héloïse Herschel is carrying my child.' The next day, Fleur had taught her three classes. As always, she had told the little girls in their pink tutus to imagine that a thread was drawing them up from the top of their heads all the way to heaven.

That day, Mirabelle was sitting in the office of her boss who, without directly blaming her for the failure of the Vaveet all-surface sponge campaign, had asked her, mildly, what her dream profession might be. He had then immediately stopped her short, to confide that he would have liked to be a singer in an English pop group. Sell millions of albums. Receive love letters in every language. 'And you, what's your greatest regret?' Mirabelle had replied that she had no regrets, no, not one, certainly not wanting to be a rock singer, nor any other flashy option, then she said that her phone was ringing in her handbag for the third time. Exasperated, Varela gestured to her to answer it. 'I don't know how to tell you this, Mirabelle. You're going to be horrified. Héloïse is pregnant.' And after a short silence to muster the courage he had lacked a second ago: 'With my child.' Mirabelle looked at Varela, at his paunch squeezed into a shiny shirt, his houndstooth tie, the spark of cruelty in his blue eyes grown weary of opening, with every blink, on the same, ordinary life. For a second she pictured him bare to the waist, deified by the spotlights' superhuman aura, crooning English words into the microphone – and at his feet, the forest of mouths and arms reaching out to his erotic glamour. Mirabelle caught sight of her own face reflected in the screen of her sleeping computer. A terrible word had slipped into her head.

Violette was kneeling in front of her open wardrobe, busy sorting through clothes, the vestiges of perfect seasons, enhanced by memory's romantic lies, when the telephone began to ring. Long, slow, loud, cinematic rings, intercut with silence. ('Lawrence has got Héloïse pregnant. They are going to have a baby.') Violette had taken a Stanley knife to the kimono Lawrence had bought for her in Tokyo and shredded it. The blade had sliced through the pool, the carp, the pagoda, the Japanese lady's legs and the head of the traitor who had promised her eternal snow.

Baptiste had snapped his bow, snatched his cello up by the

neck intending to smash it against the wall, and held back at the last minute.

Barnabé had been nauseous, with intense pains in the lower right area of his stomach, and had to have his appendix out.

When Krishna turned one, Héloïse and Lawrence left the steel and concrete cuboid they were renting in Brooklyn to set up home in a maroon brick townhouse in Greenwich Village. Every Thursday, Héloïse had lunch with Adam Atalleph, the art critic who decided who was up, who was down, and who should be keeping a weather eye on their laurels. The day after the private view of NAILS, he had published five articles, five lovesick encomia to the glory of Héloïse Herschel, and had spoken to important galleries in New York and Los Angeles on her behalf. Her work on show everywhere, Héloïse skipped the stages of misunderstood genius, poverty and torment: she made her debut at the top of the pile. Erudite critics saw similarities with photographers and painters of whom she had never heard. Collectors discerned in her the eccentric and meticulous soul of a true collector. The aesthetes who decorated their apartments with art that matched the curtains were wild about her taste for bright colours. Sociology students, feminists, *Eat & Fuck*'s readers and the lefties among the democrat sympathisers raved about this subversive new angel. When they saw Héloïse's face in the papers, romantics – along with a fair proportion of every other type of person – fell in love: a classic frenzy over beauty. Peggy Hopkins, a republican journalist and the self-satisfied wife of an evangelical pastor, railed about the 'provocative works of a single mother only twenty years old, just come over from France, her atheist country, but already trying to teach us some lessons – and ignorantly dabbling in the complex themes of incest, consumer society, the right to bear arms, the traditional American family, nationhood and racism.' Maxie Holsen asked Héloïse to marry her in *Eat & Fuck*. In his philosophy thesis titled 'Political discourse and the performative power of vision: contrary readings of Judith Butler and Héloïse Herschel', Mig Hao-To, a student at New York University, devoted 474 pages to the *Famille* ('Family'), *Fours* ('Ovens') and *Animal domestique* ('Pet') series. As for Hozumi, he had pains in his stomach, feelings of repugnance, abandonment and unfairness, but refused to diagnose them as symptoms of jealousy.

Adam Atalleph had bought *L'Amour conjugal* ('Married Love') and *Les Enfants III* ('Children III') in the period before the pricetags on Héloïse's works reached their dizzying peaks. When he was drunk, he would squeeze Héloïse's hand in both of his and tell her that he loved her, that she was his Jewish island, the only woman he would like to clasp naked in his arms and with whom he would feel free to weep. Adam lived with Viktor, a twenty-year-old student from Germany – and thirty years his junior. Blonde, tall, delicate, poised, an ear of wheat. Viktor was writing a memoir of his grandfather, a dedicated supporter of the Third Reich and the architect in charge of constructing the first cremation oven at the camp of Neuengamme, completed in April 1942. Viktor had given up both first name and surname. He called himself Rosa Winkel. He signed his undergrad history of art essays 'Rosa Winkel'. He liked this feminine name, so gentle on the tongue. The 'Rosa Winkel' referred to the pink triangle worn by homosexual prisoners in the Nazi camps. In the summer, Rosa sported a bodice with 'MY GRANDDAD BUILT AN OVEN FOR JEWS' inscribed on it in cross stitch. In the winter, he embroidered the same slogan across the back of his long wool coat in stem stitch. Rosa became Héloïse's muse. The hero of her photos, throughout her career. In the series entitled *Fours* ('Ovens'), Rosa posed in a smoking jacket with broad black and white stripes in front of the bread oven of a Pennsylvanian Amish congregation; before the aisle of microwave ovens in an electrics wholesaler in New Jersey; in front of the crematorium in Ferncliff cemetery, Westchester county; in front of the wooden cooker from Krishna's doll's house; in front of the pizza oven in a Sicilian restaurant on Mulberry Street; in front of the former foundry that was the Shark Gallery in Brooklyn; outside the human oven created by his grandfather in Neuengamme, on the banks of the Elbe. Héloïse made Krishna pose in front of the same ovens in a playsuit with wide black and white stripes. Lawrence said it wasn't right to involve the child. Héloïse took her photos smoothly, dispassionately and with great concentration. At night she thought about Auschwitz-Birkenau. Her tears fell straight from her eyes to her heart, behind the mask of her face. When she was little, a television documentary, recorded to video and watched in secret. Caught in the act. One burning cheek: her father had slapped her. Those bony faces, outsize eyes ready to fall from their sockets, were watching Héloïse and Baptiste in their French living room, on the other side of the television. Baptiste hadn't said a word. No explanation. Auschwitz-Birkenau. It was a slap from her father. Héloïse had read things. She could see. The room for undressing. Those who undressed. Shoes, more than anything. Hooks on the wall and, above each hook, a stencilled number. The voice of the SS saying in their language: 'Learn your number by heart.' The gas chamber. Not a 'chamber' at all, actually. A great cellar without any windows, just long concrete walls and steel girders. She saw them go in. Their eyes. Their belly buttons. The belly buttons that went in and the rarer ones that poked out. She could see the voice of the SS say in their language: 'Wait for the water to come.' The imaginary water. The solid sound of the hermetic door. The cast-iron canisters of Zyklon B. The red, white and black label on the Zyklon B canister and the skull on the emblem in the middle. She saw men scream and women scream, claw at themselves, tear each other to pieces, climb over each other inside the gas chamber, fighting for air, as high as they could go. She watched ten minutes go by. She saw Time. She saw the white breath of the ventilation system. She saw the overseer open the door. The sculpture of dead bodies piled right up to the ceiling, squashed up against the door – and it was as if she were again seeing the bodies clawing and tearing at themselves, and climbing upon each other desperate for air, as high as they could, towards the door. She saw the Sonderkommandos' men dragging the corpses along outside the gas chambers. The razors shaving the dead women's heads. The fingers pulling off rings and earrings. Fingers opening mouths to look for gold teeth. The dentists pulling out gold teeth with pliers. She saw the pliers. The ovens. The mass graves. The thick stench of skin and organs. She saw with all the goodness of her soul. She was not Rosa Winkel. She had no grandfather to hate, no personal monster. She had impulses of human feeling. A grief as hard as diamond.

*

Krishna screams. Koko slips into the turtle pond. Koko drinks his fill. Héloïse comes running. The hand, the whole arm plunged in. The long leash snakes along the water's surface and vanishes. Koko is drowning, Koko has drowned. Krishna sobs into Héloïse's breasts. The warmth. The scent of his neck. The heaven of sadness and kisses in his hair.

XII

Pierre Klein, the anaesthetist, has called Lawrence in New York to tell him the news. The red-head, the old lady who used to parade her batty old mug and wedding dress around the Emergency section waiting room, has been found in the car park of the Robert-Koch Paediatric Hospital. She had hidden herself, dying swan fashion, so as to die unseen between the bins with blue lids. Everyone felt her absence. She had always been there, like the pharmaceutical smell of the blue lino, like the sculpture in the waiting room (a spray of bronze spurting between two instant coffee and hot chocolate vending machines), like the bluebells that poke their way up through the car park potholes in the spring. The red-head would never die. With every season's advent she remained a newly-wed. The girl who served in the cafeteria, the interns, the doctors and the nurses collected cash in a baby's bottle to cover the funeral costs. Krishna stayed in New York. He spent the week with his sister Justine, who fed him on macadamia nut ice cream. Pierre Klein was waiting for Lawrence and Héloïse at Roissy airport, with a funereal smile. He said the red-head's name, which none of them had ever known. Lawrence was not surprised. Héloïse said: 'It's a small world.'

*

The red-head had been buried in her wedding dress, her face covered with her torn veil and, on her chest, the portrait of Hans-Jakob in German uniform that was found in the pocket of her anorak when they looked through it – the ostrich feathers did not make it to the funeral.

XIII

As soon as the last green leaf on the cherry tree, seen through the sash window, turned to gold and was relinquished, Lawrence sent the conclusions of his report on the emergency services of the hospitals of New York and New Jersey to France's Ministry of Health. With a thrill like the touch of wet snow on the back of his neck, he went into retirement. Lawrence had an innate instinct for idleness. He knew, without ever having tried them, the choreographies of the everyday. Now and then he had a twinge of angst. He thought: *That's what it is.* Aiming a baseball into Krishna's leather glove, enormous on the end of the thin white arm. Buying Velcro trainers and working them onto feet wriggling in gratefulness. Simulating an aerial attack of shampoo bottles on the bath overflowing with bubbles. Going into raptures over Krishna's drawings, little men without arms, abstract animals, flowers with electric-shock hairdos. Queuing under glowing photos of hamburgers and giant donuts, breathing in the miasma of greasy fries while explaining to Krishna that Mr McDonald's 'Happy Meal' is a deadly poison. Scooping out a pumpkin, scoring triangular eyes and a toothy mouth into its skin, inserting a candle, lighting the wick, setting the grimacing gourd on the window ledge, and watching the amber glimmerings of Halloween dancing down the street as far as he could see. Undertaking a pilgrimage to the pond where Koko went down, pretending to think suitably grave thoughts and, to console Krishna, inventing a heaven where drowned toys play at sack races and hold feasts of sweets. Once more, Lawrence felt that twinge. That's what it was. Happiness was not an electric shock. Not a divine chomp on Adam's apple. Happiness could come and go unseen.

The cherry tree lost all its leaves, bent deeply beneath the snow and rose again with pink blossoms. It was spring.

Lawrence is trying to get a spoonful of purée into Marine's tightly shut mouth. She wriggles and the scalding contents of the bendy spoon pour onto her great bare breasts. Marine is thirty-five. Lawrence awakes as if from a fall. The bedroom is sunk in the milky darkness of the small hours. 05:40 in red bars. Héloïse is sleeping soundlessly. Lawrence, lying on his back, mummified in the white sheets, weeps, and his tears sound like insect rustlings as they drip into his ears. He has not taken care of Marine and Justine. He knows nothing of their childhood selves. Therefore he can never know them. Everything he did not see then is lost. The first syllables, first *pa-pa*, unsteady steps – lost. Chickenpox – lost. Gone: that fall from the bicycle on rue de Rivoli. How could he have lost so many things? Did he throw them, still alive, imploring, into that great ravenous maw of a hospital furnace? How many years has he spent looking after nameless children? Soothing them under the false ceilings of Emergencies, crouching down to their height, saying your *maman* . . . , your *papa* . . . Is he Marine and Justine's *papa*? He is only their father. *Papa* is the affectionate name for a father, for the father's body, his anger and his kisses. Father is *papa*'s ghost. *If I had made different choices. If I had taken the time to.* That torturous *if.* Lawrence should have. To lose himself in Marine and Justine's brambly thickets; visit their cabins, their wild places. Dress up in the severe but affectionate costume of their *papa.* Force himself. Halt his personal machine, tread water, become patient, be happy to be bored, lose precious hours, spend wearisome hours. And find joy in this capitulation. Lawrence loves the minutes' slow passing when he's with Krishna. It's like a time hidden outside time. A vast time, even in its tiniest crannies, the minuscule fractions of present. Krishna smashes the galloping clock to smithereens. 05:49 on the radio-alarm. Lawrence recalls their family holidays. Marine and Justine's dresses. Their hues of apricot and roast chicken. He used to do his level best to disappear. He would count down the days, picturing the blessed moment of their return; would seek out excuses to cut the holiday short, resign himself to it at last, stay on to the very end. Except once, to join Violette in Paris, pinned between the thighs of a hot August, a storm, without an umbrella, the rain red on the fabric of her dress, sodden, *soaked* as he said to himself in English, her pretty breasts through the material, their nipples, the sudden brightening of the uncertain sky, the rainbow of their seven emotions, Violette's outline eroded by light and the great empty street throbbing with rain. It was always Fleur who organised the holidays. She would rent a house abroad: in Morocco, the States, in Italy. Or in Ireland, to please Lawrence, so she said. One year they had spent the summer on a yacht on the Croatian Adriatic. Fleur had invited a couple of friends and their children, who were the same age as Marine and Justine. Four children, two pairs of parents: a nightmare on water. Imprisoned afloat. Predictable conversations. Polite arguments with the other couple. Disagreement over the planning of each day, disagreement over the creeks they should swim in, disagreement over the ports where they'd stay the night. Screaming battles with Marine and Justine. Rudeness. Matching slaps. Regrets. The good parent's guide: never hit your children. Especially not in front of other parents. Cultural outings. Diocletian's Palace. An amphitheatre. Roman ruins. Lacking *anything* that might allow him to take pleasure in the ruins. You need energy to succeed in appreciating ruins. Imagination; erudition; or joy. Or you need to be in love. Be here with someone else. Squeeze her bottom – and the ruins are transformed. Meals: a drag. Red wine: soft drugs. Scorching days. Yawning, chatting, buzzing, drops of sweat, unhealthy sea. Taking part in conversations. Privately Fleur fumes beneath the mainsail: 'Lawrence, you read your book in your corner, you don't utter a word, this is *so* rude to our friends! *So* rude.' The damning inflexion expressed in muted fury. No respite. Children: arguments, tantrums, negotiations. Family contentment. Prison. Virgil's *Georgics*: 'High time to unyoke the steaming necks of our horses.' Make the night come. The possibility of stars. They sleep, they're in bed. Tilala is waiting for me in the cabin. I think the smell of her skin has changed. She used to have an enchanting scent.

The years, the decades have passed. The bridge, the mainmast and the half-moon. The minimal, confident singing of the swell. The temperate hour of revery. The hospital. Last Monday, a little boy, twenty months old. Diagnosed with meningitis. *In extremis*. A life saved. The new brunette intern.

And that student working on her terrible thesis. Very fine teeth. Disarming smile. Such an appropriate expression: a smile that makes you lay down all weapons, that takes away your defences. After a meeting, Sarah tells me, flushed with courage: 'I'm ready, whenever you like.' I pretend not to notice, I congratulate her on the fascinating issues raised in her introduction; I say that I'm looking forward to reading the next chapter. She shakes my hand, a vexed flick of the wrist. She leaves my office. Never a student. Golden rule. Or only *in your daydreams*. Fantasy: letting Sarah go ahead, smile at me, disarm me, undress me, tie my wrists to the bedposts, blindfold me, slip her raspberry pink tongue deep into my mouth. Sarah, if only in my fantasy, over to you. The stars. The mainmast and the half-moon shrouded in russet clouds. Forget the day, little by little. The arguments. The ruins. Fleur's sighs. And remember Fleur, *en pointe*, that very first time at the Opéra. She was the Lilac Fairy in *Sleeping Beauty*. Love at first sight. *Coup de foudre* – absolutely. Love the very instant my eye saw Fleur. In her tutu. She shied away. Refused my invitations to dinner. I called her Tilala. It was the sound of her tongue on the roof of her mouth when she said no to me.

'Will you come up and share a last glass with me?'

'Ti-la-la . . .'

That complicated first kiss. Fleur wept and pushed me away and drew me to her. Her black eyes accusing me of the dramas still to come. She had said: 'You must cause pain.' It was neither a supposition nor an order – but a prophecy. The thoughts, memories, strange regrets, on the bridge of the yacht, gently swaying, the black froth of midnight. A fissure of freedom. All thoughts allowed. An hour of lucidity, transparent and cruel.

Dare to articulate the thought from which there is no return: I hate this family life, I am stuck and bored. I stay with Tilala because it's the option that least upsets my naturally tormented disposition. I stay with Tilala because we have two children. I stay with Tilala because elsewhere the grass will be the same shade of green. I stay with Tilala because the guilt will be too great *if*. I stay with Tilala because she has inherited her father's industrial empire. She is rich. Thanks to her, I live in delightful luxury. In the morning, I open my bedroom's heavy curtains and my eyes wander the sandy paths of the Tuileries gardens. I stay with Tilala because she allows me to stray. She knows exactly how far from her I have gone. She knows how many mouths I kiss just to take me even further away. But a cynical and almost loving contract binds us: I will never abandon her.

For twenty years, Fleur has looked after everything. Lawrence has always heard summaries. Round-ups of days in the third person singular.

'Justine put her big toe in her mouth.'

'Marine lost her blankie in the Tuileries.'

'Justine said "snail".'

'Marine was sick and I called Dr Souris.'

'Justine managed to count up to eight, though she missed out number four.'

'Marine cut off another little girl's plait in the playground. I've a meeting with the headmistress.'

'Justine has done a drawing of you with a cape, a sword and a stethoscope. It's on your desk.'

'Marine has a boyfriend, I saw them kissing. They weren't too shy about it either.'

'Justine has cut her hair to a grade two all over – you should see what she's done! She looks like a sailor.'

'Marine wants to start on the pill. I told her I'd speak to you and you would say yes.'

Lawrence had said no. 'Out of the question that my baby, hardly born and about whom I know nothing, should go and fuck some young idiot.'

By leaving Fleur, Lawrence had broken his promise. Not the one mumbled in front of the mayor who lisped and wore a long-serving dusty-red carnation in his buttonhole. The one he had made to himself. He kissed Krishna's knee to make the pain go away. Krishna bounced off again singing all the way along the turtle pond where Koko had sunk in the spring. His piping voice climbed through the branches of the cherry trees.

> *Yankee Doodle went to town*
> *Riding on a pony*
> *Stuck a feather in his hat*
> *And called it macaroni!*

Lawrence gazed after the mesmerising, bird-like voice that resonated in tones of pure Héloïse. He took Krishna to a restaurant where only the little boy's head appeared above the checked tablecloth, and father and son engaged in long, thoroughly argued debates about the relative strengths of Spiderman and Tyrannosaurus rex. Meanwhile, Héloïse was travelling the length and breadth of the heavens to catch up with her photos. There had been good publicity from the big galleries in Berlin. Piles of shiny catalogues. *Héloïse Herschel. Haushaltsgeräte.* ('Héloïse

Herschel. Domestic appliances.') Héloïse caught planes and bought their replicas in miniature in the airports' duty-free zones. She closed her eyes during the dramatic accelerations, her nails digging into the fabric of the armrests. The other passengers did not seem as concerned as she was at the risk of exploding in mid-air. When Héloïse came to Paris, Mirabelle prepared by tidying beyond the requirements of order and cleanliness. She hid things in drawers and cupboards. The kitchen reeked of symmetry, wasted effort and eucalyptus detergent. The rough, pale pink towel embroidered with Héloïse's initials folded, as ever, on one side of the bidet. Héloïse flicked through the photos on the screen of her digital camera. Mirabelle asked her to slow down and, each time the frozen, full-colour face of Krishna appeared, complained about not being there to see her grandson grow up. Krishna was brown, smiling, the look in his eyes sad and distant, like his father. His head thrust into a cap with a long visor.

'He looks like a little American.'

'Mum, he is a little American.'

Mirabelle saw Héloïse's life in a six by five centimetre rectangle. She squinted to take in the house in Greenwich Village, the five steps up to the door and the turtle-shaped knocker. 'You seem very nicely set up. And I love the tree! Is it a cherry?' Each photo was a view through a keyhole: her daughter's secret life. And these unfamiliar faces, laughing silently in her photos, leaning drunkenly on Héloïse's shoulder, in her living room, in her kitchen, somewhere else, eyes red and narrowed against the flash, new friends, artists perhaps, Mirabelle did not ask. Lawrence was losing his hair. In several of the photos, his pink scalp could be seen between ash-grey clumps. The bags beneath his large eyes had deepened. Little russet marks had appeared on his cheeks and neck. Mirabelle no longer used his name. The word stuck in her throat like a great unchewed mouthful of steak. She called him 'the father'. 'How is the father doing?' With the sting clear in her ironic tone.

At Roissy airport, Héloïse hesitated between two miniature aeroplanes. She chose the Airbus A318. At worst, Krishna would end up with two the same. Through the porthole, she watched the bridal veil trailing behind a plane below, in the slow, paradise-blue sky. She pictured the people sitting inside that other airborne toy. Their worried eyes when they lifted the foil lid and discovered the 'salmon steak with tagliatelli and its spring vegetables' in the middle of a meal-tray divided into silver-coloured geometric sections. The man sitting next to Héloïse – a tall blonde guy she'd stared at in the departure lounge – poked his fork into the brown, right-angled dessert. Before kissing Héloïse and handing her suitcase over, Lawrence had said: 'Look at you, my beautiful lion, you're on the other side.' She heard his words again and tears came to her eyes. At every departure she hugged Lawrence tightly as if for the last time. She used to be gripped by the same panic in those days when she would run up the stairs to the forbidden eyrie on rue des Martyrs. It was perpetually the end and the last of their kisses. Héloïse was on the other side. Even holding each other tight, the forty years were a torrent between their stricken shores. She counted on her fingers. Soon it would be ten years together. The star-canopied beach at the far edge of the garden, behind the screen of cactus and pines, the silvery whispering of the rosemary, the cool grains of sand, rough under her knees.

Lawrence's penis in her thirteen-year-old hand. The biggest penis in the world. Though later, with other lovers, Héloïse saw that Lawrence's penis was not in the least outsized. Hozumi's was bigger, topped with a big, broad-edged glans not unlike a Napoleonic cocked hat. Rosa Winkel's penis was longer and had a bend in it. Vadim's was hard like a raw potato. The man beside Héloïse tipped custard from his walnut-studded rhomboid onto their shared armrest. Héloïse rummaged in her handbag. Tissues. Responding blushes. Dimples in his smile.

'Thanks . . . I'm such a klutz. Thanks . . . Sorry . . . Such an idiot . . . I've got some on your . . .'

'No! Not even a drop . . .'

'I don't think it will stain . . . custard . . . Wait. Can I give you something for . . . just a sec . . . for the dry-cleaning?'

'What are you thinking? Fifty dollars! You should get a new dry-cleaner . . .'

'Yes, I really should . . . One time, I lost the slip they give you to get your things back – and the owner didn't even want to know! Even though I'd been there I don't know how many times before . . . but nothing doing . . . even though I used to go every two or three weeks . . . Don't know why I'm telling you that, it's not interesting . . .'

'Are you going to Boston for work?'

'Yes, but first I have to get myself set up there. I need to buy furniture, all the electrical things . . . The apartment is empty. I wanted a furnished one . . . It's impersonal . . . it's . . . Before, I used to go back and forth. I was always either in Boston or Paris . . . I used to stay at the Holiday Inn . . . Not great . . . Have you ever . . . ? But I'm not going to bore you silly with my tales right away . . . Do you live in Boston?'

'No, I live in New York. I'm going to Boston for a photo exhibition.'

'You're studying photography?'

'I've never studied anything . . . I don't even have my Baccalaureate.'

'Ah well that's not . . . qualifications . . . they don't do much . . . Well, I did law . . . Commercial law at Paris X Nanterre . . . For the last two years I've been working at a legal firm. Brown & Minkowski . . . Don't imagine you've heard of it?'

'Do you wear that black nightgown with the white thing?'

'Oh no! You see, I don't enter pleas in court. I advise companies on points of law . . . over money issues . . . But you know, they're not nightgowns . . .'

'Where do you buy them? I've always wondered.'

'Err . . . There are specialist shops . . . Mostly we get them tailored to fit . . .'

'Isn't it a problem in your line of work to be so shy and go red like that all the time?'

'Excuse me. You should never say . . .'

'What?'

'Never tell someone who's blushing that they're blushing.'

'Why?'

'They'll die of embarrassment. Don't you ever blush?'

'No.'

It was when Héloïse pronounced that unadorned, untruthful 'no' that Héloïse Herschel and Vadim Verkhovsky felt the desire to kiss.

XIV

The Ford is slowly making its way through the residential area of Beacon Hill. The brick facades, the strips of turf, the shimmering pink air, the undulations of bow windows in the red dawn light. It will be a fine day. Héloïse's phone rings. The car brakes suddenly to avoid a dog. The driver directs a stream of Hindi insults at the very slow, almost deaf cocker spaniel, which stops in the middle of the road to sniff at a brown turd.

'I'm in the taxi, now . . .'

'Héloïse! I've been calling you all night!'

'I'm in the taxi. I'll call you from the airport.'

'You know what time it is? You'll miss your flight!'

'I'll catch the next one.'

'Are you with the press officer? With Marty?'

'No, I'm by myself . . . They had more people to see in Boston for the June show. They'll join me on Tuesday.'

'You're alone in Los Angeles 'til Tuesday? Was that the plan?'

'Yes, that was the plan . . . Lawrence . . . Stop worrying!'

'Do you want me to come over? I'm coming . . . I'll leave Krishna with Justine and I'll—'

'No! I'll have hundreds of things to sort out! I have to supervise the hang . . . The gallery's enormous . . . The rooms are 100 metres square . . . My photos will be lost in all that space . . .'

'I must have called you fifty times. Where were you?'

'I left my phone in the hotel bathroom.'

'Why didn't you borrow someone's phone so you could call me?'

'I don't know your number by heart.'

'Then learn it! Dammit! I was out of my mind with worry!'

'Lawrence, I'm sorry . . . I didn't realise . . .'

'I've been calling you all night! What time did you get back to the hotel?'

'Late. It was complicated . . . Marty spent an hour on the phone with the insurers . . . There's a problem with five photos from the *Deuxième Amendement* series . . . They're not in the insurer's contract, I've no idea why . . . Anyway, the girl who runs the gallery in LA refused to put them up . . . Afterwards we invited the gallery people to a restaurant to say thank you . . . Then they took us to a bar, to thank us for taking them out for dinner . . . I drank four Brain Attacks . . . four . . . I really shouldn't have . . . It's this disgusting kind of cocktail: gin-and-vodka-and-Malibu-and-Kahlua . . . I wanted to call you then and that's when I realised I didn't have my phone . . . I thought I'd left it at the gallery . . . It was too late to go back and Marty wanted to go dancing . . . We ended up in an '80s nightclub, a super-kitsch rock gig . . . The singer had a denim jacket completely covered in safety pins. My press officer started making out with the bassist . . . Marty flirted with the singer . . . The guy called him gay . . . Marty tapped him on the bum . . . They started hitting each other and we were all thrown out . . . Marty insulted the bouncer, who punched him in the belly . . . well . . . not a real punch . . . barely a slap, but it knocked Marty to the ground . . . He wanted us to take him to hospital, said he had internal bleeding. The press girl was so drunk she wet herself . . . The taxis wouldn't take us . . . Well, one did but the guy made us get out in the next street because we were too wrecked . . . We walked home in the end . . . An hour and a half . . . I must have reached the hotel around five . . . I set my alarm for half past . . . Didn't hear a thing when it went off . . .'

'Héloïse?'

'What?'

'Don't do this again.'

'I'm sorry if you were worried . . . Is Krishna up?'

'Not yet.'

'Tuesday . . . You won't forget his recorder for school, will you?'

'Just call me from the airport.'

Héloïse stows her phone back in her handbag. The taxi brakes abruptly at a red light. Héloïse lets her head drop onto Vadim's shoulder.

Lawrence and Krishna are very late, hurrying across the square in front of the nursery school. Lawrence forgot the recorder. At the top of the flagstaff, the American flag, freshly washed, hangs at sixty degrees. The wind picks up. The fifty stars and the red and white stripes, solidly sewn together, fly out against the pure September sky. The main door is still open. The headmistress is surrounded by parents. 'My God!' The exclamation repeated over and over. 'My God', on every face, in the hallway lined with children's drawings. Little Zoe's mother gently strokes the teacher's arm. Some mothers are crouching and hugging their children tightly. Others make phone calls, standing, leaning on the cow-, donkey- and snake-headed letters of the alphabet. Words flow into their numbed ears. They put their hands over their mouths. Ringtones jingle into each other – a cock-crow, the 'Turkish March', 'The Star-Spangled Banner', the first bars of the Rolling Stones' 'Paint It Black'. All the calls deliver the same news. Lawrence speaks to the teacher. He calls Héloïse. He hears her voice. She is in the departure lounge at Boston airport. In the corner of one classroom, two fathers are sitting in miniature chairs, next to a papier mâché queen. They don't know each other. They are holding hands.

Lawrence and Krishna re-emerge from school, going past the foot of the flagpole. 'Is everybody dead? Who is going to fix the broken houses?' Lawrence doesn't answer. He moves with great strides, forcing Krishna to hurry. (*Héloïse can't have left her phone in the hotel bathroom. She called me in the middle of the afternoon when she was already at the gallery. Why would she have gone back to the hotel. So she could change for the evening, have a bath. And that's when she'd have left her phone beside the basin. Go back to the hotel just to get changed. Take a bath in the middle of the day. Héloïse does not wash in the middle of the day. I tell her I tried to call her all night and she replies that the press officer has wet herself. There's a metro in Boston. It runs all night. Why all the details? She gave the recipe of the cocktail she was drinking. Doesn't listing the components of a cocktail amount to saying I spent the night with someone. Héloïse sleeps lightly. She hears her alarm go off. She finds departures stressful. She always gets to the airport an hour and a half early and clenches her jaw teeth-grindingly tightly when the plane takes off. Héloïse is lying to me.*)

Lawrence decides to drop Krishna off with Justine. She has put on weight. Her stomach chastens from under a T-shirt showing Homer Simpson strangling a cat. Justine stinks of alcohol. Her eyes are red-marbled; fresh tears mingle with salty crystalline traces marking the paths of older tears. Lawrence draws her into his arms.

'It's terrible, sweetheart . . .'

'What are you talking about?'

'The planes . . .'

Justine has not heard the news. She is crying because Maxie has left her for Betty Lost, the guitarist in Funny Paedophile. Justine wants to go back to Paris. She wants to live in Montmartre. She wants a paved courtyard and pots of scented herbs on the kitchen window ledge. She wants to go out with a normal girl. An English teacher or an architect. A Sophie or a Céline. She wants to adopt an African baby. With little brown nails. She wants to stop photographing nails. She wants to photograph weddings, baptisms, pregnant women, primary school classes. She wants to eat sensibly. She wants to go to bed early. She wants to join a gym. She wants to read the masterpieces of classical literature. She wants to stop smoking. No. She needs to smoke. She wants to stop drinking. She doesn't need to drink.

'*Papa*, do you think I smell of alcohol?'

'A little.'

'I'm sick of everything.'

'Do you know what a Brain Attack is?'

'Kahlua-Malibu-gin-and-vodka. Carnage.'

XV

It has a dome and crystal chandeliers (let's say it's a room for holding receptions, empty, with waxed floors, looking out over a French-style garden, perhaps belonging to an embassy). A fresco on the inside of the dome: chubby-legged cherubim and great dumb stretches of sky. Beneath the dome, nineteen corpses dressed as drowned women, still dripping seawater (it's all fake; put there for the photos). The women's faces are coated in creamy white make-up, like that worn by clowns or geishas. Their hair shines with black wax. Their skirts, jackets and shoes have steeped for two days and two nights in olive oil. Damp compresses have been stuffed under eyelids (Héloïse saw to this). And golfballs inside cheeks. Mouths mime burlesque and statuesque agonies. Standing at the summit of the human heap, in a beige suit and butter-coloured gloves, Rosa Winkel gives a deliberately unnatural smile. Her brand new loafers rest upon two heads (Mina and Lucy, two biology students who sometimes pose for Héloïse – to keep the wolf from the door). The photo is shot from below: in the background, the cherubim puff out their pink cheeks.

Drowned Women is hanging in the gallery's main room. The exhibition, entitled *Survivor Syndrome*, stretches the length of a windowless, air-conditioned white corridor. Outside, July is suffocating Paris. After *Drowned Women* come *Burned Women*, *Shaken Women*, *The Women Conscripts*, *HIV-Positive Women*, *Women Capsized*, *Bombed Women*, *Starving Women*, *Women Casualties of the A8 Highway*, *Raped Women*, *The Plague*, *Kidnapped Women*, *Irradiated Women*, *Mushrooms*, *Soaked Women*, *Shot Women*, *Gassed Women*, *Fallen Women* and *The Chosen Woman*, with which the exhibition concludes.

Barnabé reads the text printed on the white wall, which runs over into *Drowned Women*.

Survivor Syndrome refers to the post-traumatic shock that can affect those who have survived situations of extreme gravity. The syndrome may be manifest particularly as a powerful sense of guilt at being alive while others have died.

Last September 11, Héloïse Herschel should have been on board the Boeing 767 that left Boston's Logan International Airport at 07:59 and crashed into the North Tower of the World Trade Center at 08:46. She missed her flight.

Héloïse had left Gallery 555 by the back door at around seven in the evening, in a red dress, on 10 September 2001. Marty had caught up with her halfway down the spiral of the emergency staircase. (Marty is the meticulous, touchy secretary who organises everything so that Héloïse doesn't need to worry about anything.) Marty had squeezed Héloïse's wrist and whispered everything he'd said. ('Everyone's waiting for you! Don't tell me you're leaving! You've lost it! This isn't eccentric any more, it's rude!') Marty had said that the gallery's people were doing a superb job for Héloïse and that the least she could do was . . . At that, Héloïse had cut him short with a doubtful smile ('They've been raking it in thanks to me'). Marty had said, more threateningly, that they had arranged a farewell buffet especially for her, with sushi and exorbitantly expensive champagne. Héloïse had refrained from saying that she could no longer stand sushi since Hozumi had made her try raw eel with wasabi. 'It would be an exceptionally serious professional mistake not to stay and dine with everyone on your last evening in Boston.' (Marty was going red in the face.) Héloïse, who occasionally could be perfectly irritating, had said, calmly: 'All right then, Marty, I'm committing an exceptionally serious professional mistake.' Marty had pointed at her red bodice, the shameless, barely there dress. 'You know what you are? A little trollop all puffed up with success!' Words you would never have thought to hear from the diplomatic and decorous lips of the loyal secretary. Even Héloïse had felt uneasy; perhaps not remorseful, but a hint of moral discomfort, the first naggings of culpability – yet Vadim was waiting for her, arms crossed, at the bottom of the spiral staircase.

Making love to Vadim meant lying down. Vadim would kiss her feet and then, unhurriedly, make his way back upstream, along the naked river. The journey along the calves was long and boring. The strange skin of the knees. What does pleasure require? The slow thighs, scarcely touched. Héloïse wants to grab a fistful of that blonde hair, uproot the studious mouth and plant it in the midstream of her erotic lava. Instead, she would let him handle her. Not moving. The subtlety of sexual pleasure. A millimetre. A second. A scent. The pleasure that hangs by a thread. The infinitely small.

His mouth brushes her mons Veneris and retreats. Héloïse moans with hope and disappointment. Vadim climbs back, kiss by kiss, up the impatient, quivering stomach. Soon his snail mouth will trail its stickiness along Héloïse's armpits. Later, her breasts will be nibbled. After an eternity, the languid, penitent penis will breaststroke into a vagina that's going crazy with frustration. Vadim is a hero. A rare case. A monster of patience. But Héloïse prefers Lawrence's shortcuts. His fierce grip. His dirty pleasures. And while an enraptured Vadim licks her clavicle, Héloïse dreams of Lawrence slapping her and spitting a love potion at her neck.

Three days and three nights with Vadim, until the morning of 11 September. Really, it was terribly sweet, the stream of incomplete caresses. At five in the morning, Héloïse had felt cold. Vadim had lent her a Brown & Minkowski T-shirt which smelled of his coffee and burnt-sugar skin. She had slipped it on, then taken it off shortly after, tugging at her lover's arm as it dangled from the bed.

'Héloïse, stop! If we don't leave the flat in less than seven minutes, you'll miss it. I don't mind—'

'Stay in bed.'

'I know the way really well . . . It's at least forty minutes door to door and there could be traffic around the airport. Besides, I have to be at the office by half past eight because at nine the assistant director—'

'Come on. I'll teach you a new way to fuck.'

'Hey! Take it easy, expert! Perhaps I know your new way already, miss; after all, I have—'

'You don't know it. It's called quickly and badly. (It's the opposite of your philosophy of the arsehole.)'

Barnabé stops for a long time in front of *Mushrooms*. A gleaming, ad-world kitchen. The family sit at the table. The three young children and their father are dead, heads toppled into their fried vegetables. Only the mother (Rosa Winkel), with her polite smile, brown wig and fetching apron, has finished her plate and is burying her last forkful inside her prettily lipsticked mouth. Violette comes up beside Barnabé and, applying every kilo of her minimal weight, attaches herself to his arm.

'I'm looking round her photos . . . I'd love to ask her . . .'

'Do you want her to give you a photo? She'll give you as many as you want.'

'No, I want her to photograph me.'

'*Maman*, not now . . . You're too tired . . .'

'If I pose for Héloïse, I'll be making art out of shit. And all this shit has to be good for something. When I woke up this morning, I told myself that I need to put some poetry in my shit.'

Violette is sick. Barnabé and his wife Fanny go with her to the Pitié-Salpêtrière Hospital for her chemotherapy sessions. When the medication goes into her veins, Violette feels as if she's being poisoned. She likes *Mushrooms* so much. It's an allegory of the great betrayal: Death dressed up as a delectable supper. Violette moves slowly on to *The Chosen Woman*. All the photos have the same dimensions except for this little red-and-white, very over-exposed Polaroid. A hotel bedroom. Clothes on the floor. A couple can be made out lying in bed, but only one face is visible – that of Héloïse. Adam Atalleph has come over from New York. He is going to publish an article in *Libération*.

Héloïse is putting her muse, the eccentric Berlin performance artist Rosa Winkel, to the test. Rosa is the terrestrial angel who survives every tragedy: tsunami, car accident, epidemic, earthquake, rape, war, poisoning, concentration camp, nuclear fallout, terrorist attack. But is the Survivor even part of the tragedy? Is he even in the photo? In Fallen Women, *a photo with a hole in it, Rosa Winkel has been crudely cut out with a craft knife, extracted. Thrown from the heights of the Twin Towers, the screaming shapes fall around a Rosa Winkel who is suspended in a fatal absence; voiceless, blank, invisible. The Survivor 'wasn't there'. He resides in History's slumbers. Just as Héloïse Herschel slumbers in the incredibly simple and staggering Polaroid that marks a comma – never a full stop – beside this Chosen Woman's guilty conscience.*

Lawrence observes Héloïse. Two journalists touch her arm. She is radiant. As beautiful as he is old. As strong as he is lost. They split up that morning.

'Héloïse, I loathe treasure hunts and guessing games.'

'It's not a guessing game. They're photos. Each person sees what they see.'

'And what am I meant to see in *Chosen Woman*?'

'Nothing. You see what you see, Lawrence.'

'Stop playing games.'

'You think it's some kind of confession?'

'You're showing this photo to thousands of people! You're revealing our private life.'

'It's just a fucking photo!'

'No, Héloïse! It's a photo that says: "I didn't die in the 9/11 attacks because I was fucking in a hotel room." It's hardly brave of you, Miss Herschel, to tell me like this.'

'What's wrong with you?'

'I'm going to stay in a hotel for a while.'

'You want to leave me? Because of this shitty little photo?'

'Because of everything. You're too far away. You're too beautiful. You're always hurting me.'

'I'm always hurting you?'

'You can't help it. It's your beauty and your strength that hurt me.'

'You're leaving me? Now?'

'You've been leaving me bit by bit for the last ten years.'

'I'm in love with you, that's all!'

'That's precisely it. You're in love with me and that's all. You don't need anything more. You don't even need me to love you. You love being in love and you love the violence of your own feelings. The rest . . .'

'I don't understand what you're saying.'

Héloïse, Lawrence and Krishna had gone back to Paris eight months after the attacks. No one had asked them to leave. Raw emotion coursed through the streets of New York. People wanted to cry. They smiled at strangers. They shared the same thoughts. They dreamed the same nightmares. They made up the same lies to explain what had happened, in awful, attenuated words, to their children. They breathed the grey dust. They made many visits to the site of the wreckage. The candles; the poems tied to the wire fence; the photos. These ruins were nothing like the Roman ruins that bored Lawrence. These were powerful ruins. They bled. Yet never had Héloïse and Lawrence felt so foreign. These were not their towers. Their arms had not been torn off. They were grieved to plumb this dark night of the soul, but they had lost neither limbs nor their pride. Something intangible put them at a distance. They were not American.

Héloïse did not know Kelly Morgan well. When this tall, vapid and athletic girl had bought *Chien de famille* claiming that the Labrador's coat would go just right with the upholstery in her office, Héloïse had felt the purest contempt. But when Héloïse saw those planes strike the towers, the soundless images on the great screens in Boston's airport, she thought that, first of all, our world is visual. With its language of signs, microscopic or spectacular, made up of colours and shapes. Neither invisible nor divine, works of art are, first of all, *seen*. They exist just as the printer and the sofa in Kelly's office exist – Kelly who had been right to consider whether *Chien de famille*'s place should be on her office wall – in the midst of life and all the other objects in the world. Kelly had been a financial analyst at Cantor Fitzgerald and worked on the 102nd floor of the World Trade Center's North Tower. A Boeing 767 crashed into her tower. She died and at the very same moment her 657 colleagues at Cantor Fitzgerald died too. Héloïse recites the litany of ifs. If she had not made love with Vadim one more time, quickly and badly, she would have flown at 796 kilometres per hour into Kelly's office. They would have died side by side. The Labrador and the beige sofa would have burned along with them.

Above the Atlantic, Lawrence had felt old. The joy of youth lay not in being young but in having your whole life ahead of you and knowing it. Imagining, before any experience of them, the surprises that the future holds, that exquisite army of first times, successes, prides, encounters, diluvian joys. What more was left for him? Once more to savour the happy drug of work. To take part in symposiums in great hushed amphitheatres. To publish articles about American public hospitals. To make a proposal to the Ministry of Health for improving France's emergency services. Dip into politics. Go on being useful. Lawrence had sighed. Krishna was pressing his nose and tongue against the aeroplane window. 'Stop it Krishna! That's disgusting!' What a strange order these things were, endlessly, unthinkingly dealt out. How to know what matters? What forms a child? Which words will stay with him? Which rages will run off his skin without leaving a trace? Which imperceptible details will damage him for ever? Krishna's mouth had made a heart of condensation and bubbly saliva on the glass. Lawrence suddenly remembered Marine, in another place, licking another aeroplane window. They had been going on a family holiday to a place near Rome, a house Tilala had rented, a few kilometres from the ruins at Ostia. When Krishna was born, Marine had stopped talking to her father. He had seen her in December at the aging Jeanne's apartment. The gingerbread St Nicholases. The tree dressed up for Christmas. The buffet. And Marine sat there, on the chaise longue's Provençal design, furious. It was easy to read her thoughts. ('You abandoned *maman*. You had a baby with a baby. I shall never forgive you.') Justine (*my favourite daughter*, he thought, with a kind of relief and a painful tenderness) had stayed behind in New York alone, so as to be near Maxie Holsen and the ashes of their love. Lawrence felt her unhappiness. Something was feeding her on peanut butter and vanilla ice cream. Something was holding her in front of the hypnotic television late into the night. Something made her pour gin into herself. Something dressed her body in shapeless tracksuit bottoms. Something stopped her from sleeping at night. Lawrence wanted to know the source of her trouble. He had stopped off at her place one evening and sat down in a chair in her grimy Brooklyn kitchen, intending to have an intimate conversation. They had talked about the rising cost of apartments in New York and about Woody Allen's latest film, *Hollywood Ending* – the story of a director who loses his sight the day before the start of shooting and whose film, which is impossible to sit through, is a worldwide fiasco except in France, where they can't praise it enough. They cried with laughter. They have been living in New York long enough to know what Americans truly think of the French: pretentious, moany and eccentric out of sheer snobbery. Justine dried her tears and stuffed a few Pepperidge Farm pecan cookies into her mouth. Lawrence had watched Justine chew. He was afraid he might be the cause of her depression.

The plane is approaching Paris. The stewardess is carrying a tray of sandwiches that she offers to the passengers by leaning gracefully towards the right-hand rows, while her twin makes the same obeisances in the direction of the left-hand rows. Dancers' necks. Lawrence dreams he is ringing at Fleur's door, at the rue de Rivoli place. She is wearing her grey cashmere jumper, outsized and elegant, which leaves her neck and shoulders uncovered. Her bare feet and the crescent moon earrings he bought her in Casablanca, in the early days of their marriage. They don't say anything. They smile at each other. Lawrence lays his bag on the unchanging white lacquered console. The photo from their holiday in Croatia is still in the frame of the entrance hall mirror. Justine and Marine, golden, half naked sulky adolescents, in the bow of the yacht. He sits on the sofa. Chanel No. 5. Tilala disappears into the corridor. Through the walls, Lawrence recognises the quick rhythm of her steps. She comes back with a novel in her hand. 'It's very stupid but I can't stop crying!' A family saga that takes place in Puglia, twins separated at birth, an impossible passion, a riding accident, a terrible secret that burdens its keepers, a concealed pregnancy, a complicit cleric, buried treasure, fierce midday sun, a parcel of dry land that four brothers argue over and a great-grandmother who is, in the end, neither deaf nor dumb and who, on her deathbed, whispers the answer to every one of the mysteries. Tilala will read *Nothing New Under the Sun* at top speed, her chest agitated by visible and delightful emotion. She sits, she curls up. She picks a grey hair from his sleeve. Her cat-like delicacy. She wedges a cushion behind her back and frowns as she looks for her page. Lawrence knows her every movement. She reads. Ten minutes. Turns the pages. Interrupts herself: 'No! Bother! I'm much further in! Luigi hasn't had his riding accident yet!' Lawrence is lost in her. The bookshelves. The red section that is their photo albums. Tilala's bare feet. Happiness, perhaps. The plane is battling a squall. The cabin shakes. A melodious note. The emergency lights go on above their heads. Lawrence turns to Héloïse. She is asleep. Her long, loose hair. The strange sea-blue, American Airlines eye-mask rubs out her face. Héloïse had been rigid with fear from the moment of take-off. Her lungs couldn't take in the aeroplane air. The stewardess had rushed over to her with a cup of water and a sugar sachet. 'Breathe slowly and think about something very nice and very relaxing . . . Imagine you're swimming breaststroke in turquoise waters . . . among clownfish . . .' Lawrence had wrapped his arms around Héloïse. 'If you don't feel well, don't hesitate to call me . . . but nothing can harm you in daddy's arms!'

XVI

The lid says 'DOMESTIC GOODS' in black felt tip. Héloïse empties the cardboard box over her mother's head. Catalogues, press clippings, post from the four corners of the world mess up Mirabelle's grey fringe and fall onto the slippers with Mickey Mouse ears and tails that Héloïse brought back for her from New York. Seven years have gone by since her last *Domestic Goods* exhibition, installed beneath the magical glass roof of the Niji gallery in Kyoto. Hundreds of envelopes and email print-outs. Eulogies and rants. In every language, strangers congratulate Héloïse on her militant and poetic work. Some call her a witch, Lucifer incarnate or a feminist slut. The Italians see *Domestic Goods* as a metaphor for the alienation of modern man, metamorphosed into a machine for consumption. The Germans find in Héloïse's photos the power to breathe life into mechanised bodies that have been stripped of all joy and spirit. For a law professor at the University of Cologne, *Domestic Goods* represents a contemporary adaptation of Freud's *Three Essays on the Theory of Sexuality*. A Texan entrepreneur encloses a plane ticket with his letter inviting the 'anti-American whore' to go home. Krishna flicks through the German edition of the exhibition catalogue. The glossy paper makes each photo rustle. *Electric Crêpe Pan, Food Processor, Toaster*

I and *Toaster II, Microwave*. In *Iron*, naked and scarred by purple burns, Rosa Winkel slumbers on a downy angel's wing. In *Electric Floor-Polisher*, encased in a silver lamé dress, hanging by her feet from the blades of a ceiling fan, Rosa Winkel licks a parquet floor awash with saliva. In *Washing Machine*, a Wall Street trader in her grey suit, Rosa Winkel scrubs the bloody heart of a sheep with a bar of Marseilles soap.

Mirabelle snatches the catalogue out of Krishna's hands.

'When you're grown up!'

'I am grown up!'

Since his parents' separation, Krishna has had two bedrooms, two neighbourhoods and two front doors. He lives with Lawrence from Sunday to Thursday and with Héloïse from Thursday to Sunday. On Thursday he has to leave his father. On Sunday he has to leave his mother. Krishna's life is separations. Organised and ritual. Repeated into infinity. He often thinks of his American school, of the starry flag that touched the sky at the end of the flagpole. Krishna's teacher, Mrs Jonas, used to pin his drawings up in the classroom, even the half-finished ones and the ones that went wrong. She praised him as soon as he articulated the first sketch of an idea. She did the same with all the children. Her praise pushed their beginners' minds to come up with more drawings and more ideas. His French school was different. The threat of bad marks and the fear of saying something stupid hovered like two knives over hesitant heads. The students would retain this apprehension for the rest of their lives. It would freeze their imagination, stunt their pluckiness, amputate the limbs of their art. Krishna cries every morning. Krishna cries so much that Héloïse takes him out of school in the middle of the year and signs him up to complete his last year of primary school by correspondence. Vexed by Héloïse's decision, Lawrence sends her a letter. Every line of his evasive, illegible writing – 'doctor's writing', Fleur says – ends in a series of long, fading strokes, in which his argument seems to dissolve along with the wavering ink, beyond the reach of alphabet and decipherable loops and links.

School imitates society. It is beastly and boring. It works like a vaccine. It transmits a little beastliness and boredom into the body of the schoolchild in order that, on leaving behind the untrammelled reveries of that early golden age and discovering the adult world, the child does not die of disappointment.

Héloïse replies that the aim of any life is precisely to produce enough art and enough love to escape the boredom and the brutality of life. You might as well practise escaping youth. Reading her response, Lawrence feels a pang of regret. She has a gift for perfect excess. Her tempers, her kisses, her finely turned ideas, her volcanic delights: everything is done to excess. Héloïse, exemplary dweller in the minute and the second, in the jolt of the instant. Her imminent skin, her touch, her voice in a minor key, Aeolian. Her ingenuous, imperious way of saying: 'I've loved you since I was born!' And her high-piled hair. Lawrence leaves the living room. Bolts to the end of the corridor. In the bedroom. In the bedside cabinet. Inside the Napoleon III ebony box with flowering tendrils in brass marquetry. The thick lock of curly hair, gathered from the hospital floor in 1981.

*

Mirabelle deciphers a twelve-page letter tied together with an olive-wood rosary. Mary McKendree, the Californian collector, says she has understood who Héloïse is and also the aim of her photographic projects. Héloïse is the exterminating angel who, with her apocalyptic works, accompanies the Lord's lambs towards death and on to eternal life. Mrs McKendree adored the *Domestic Goods* exhibition. She bought *Electric Lobster Pick* for 58,000 dollars, saying she had seen the painting that had inspired *Electric Lobster Pick* in Venice. It was *St George Killing the Dragon*, on view at the Scuola di San Giorgio degli Schiavoni, Vittore Carpaccio, 1504. Mary McKendree prays Héloïse will be kind enough to confirm this intuition.

'Give her her money back! She's mad, poor thing . . .'

'She's bought five photos from me over ten years. That's more than 200,000 dollars!'

'You think it's okay, charging 200,000 dollars for bits of paper? What do you do with all that money? Is it so difficult to take a photo? How long does it take you to do, one photo?'

'That's not really the point, *maman* . . . Help me find the letter from the German who thought I was a cannibal . . .'

'The one who tried to take you to court?'

'You're mixing him up with Van Horenbeeck . . . the Belgian who thought the photo of Krishna in black-and-white striped pyjamas in the crematorium constituted incitement to infanticide and an insult to the memory of the Shoah.'

'People are so dumb.'

Héloïse is waiting for Lawrence to come back. He lets her believe he's living in their former eyrie on the rue des Martyrs. Héloïse holds herself bolt upright and, when no one is watching, she stands even straighter. As soon as she's awake, she gets away from her melancholy bed. She concentrates her knife-sharp focus on *Tunnel*, the exhibition she is preparing with her aunt Violette. She won't let her thoughts take root. She unearths the perilous seeds, tears out the weeds of regret. She avoids the past. Leonard Cohen's albums. Scarlett O'Hara and Rhett Butler. The books they used to read still in each other's arms. *Fermina Márquez. Lointain Intérieur. Cronopios and Famas. La Belle Lurette. Gone with the Wind.* When she masturbates, Héloïse bans Lawrence from her pornographic repertoire. She dreams of fucking strangers, gladiators, aliens, bulls and snakes. But every night, at about 3 A.M., she writes to Lawrence. A real letter like in the old days of letter-writing. Violette says it's healthy, a purging of love. Violette and Héloïse are alike. They believe in miracles and exceptions. In joy. Héloïse has promised Violette she will save her – and Violette does not for a second doubt Héloïse's promise. Violette is tired. Her pretty rounded cheeks are no more. Never any appetite. Not a hair left. No wish to make love. No strength to mount a horse. No left breast. A horror of mirrors. The photos in the *Tunnel* show will be in a very tiny square format. Five centimetres by five centimetres. To see every detail, your face will have to come close enough to kiss the paper. In *I Do My Hair*, Violette, dressed in a snakeskin print slip, brushes a blonde wig hanging on a butcher's hook. In *I Go Horse-Riding*, Violette carries on her back a 480 kilo piebald horse called Rhodos, the great-grandson of Cronos, who broke her wrist. In *I'm Hungry*, her spidery legs and one-eyed torso are covered in chocolate cream puffs, squid-ink spaghetti and pistachio macaroons. In *I'm Skin and Bones*, Violette wears a long tunic made out of chicken bones and cartilage. In *Where Did I Put My Breast?*, Violette wears stiletto heels as she climbs the putrid mound of a municipal rubbish dump, a voluptuous pink wax breast balanced on her hairless head. In *Here Lived a Wildly Exciting Breast According to My 79 Lovers*, Violette's great scar blushes deep red, filling the photo. In *Eat, This is My Breast*, Violette chews heartily at a silicone mammary prosthetic.

'Listen to this . . . It's funny . . .'
  'Hatemail?'
  'No . . . It's from an old American lady . . .'

Dear Mademoiselle Herschel,
  Please excuse my French: I've forgotten everything. I was fluent when I was living in Paris with Pierre, the great love of my youth. I'm a retiree and a self-taught art-lover. This is my first computer letter! I hope you receive it without a worry. My great-granddaughter Meadow (she is sitting after me) is helping me make the first steps in the computer. For the love of heaven, I do not want to look like my mother, who hated modernity and didn't know how to send the telegram or call the telephone!
  From the bottom of my heart, I adored your exhibition Domestic Goods, *in the Georges-Pompidou Centre. It's fabulous! I visited it with Meadow, during our journey to Paris. I cannot believe that you are a young woman of only 23! At your age, I was in the hole of Wisconsin with my mother who forbid me from reading Francis Scott Fitzgerald's stories and T. S. Eliot. She was a widow of the war. My father was a soldier in the first infantry division, The Big Red One. He died in the*

front in Picardy in November 1918. I want to send you by post
the badge he used to wear on his shoulder. Can I ask your
address? One day perhaps I will see my father's badge in a
photo of you, who knows?

All your photos, and in particular Electric Fryer *and*
Electric Citrus-Press, *have touched me deep in my heart. I*
can't reason why. Perhaps because I worked at one of Hoover's
vacuum cleaner factories and I obeyed men all my life. I seem
that I still have not understood the meaning of your works. But
you neither, have you?

With all my affection and the best memory of Paris,
Katherine Szalowski

Suddenly Héloïse remembers Lawrence reading *The Hunting of
the Snark* aloud in Normandy, in the hotel with the flowery
wallpaper, near the grey waves, under beige and golden skies.
He had read standing up, naked, stomach sucked in, his cock
straighter and straighter as the crew drew near the Snark. And
breaking off several times to acknowledge that the French
translation was, all things considered, remarkable. At the end
of this long poem, illustrated by Max Ernst's comical and
painstaking drawings, Lewis Carroll writes the following:

*I have received courteous letters from strangers begging to know
if* The Hunting of the Snark *is an allegory, or contains some
hidden moral, or is a political satire: and for all such questions I
have but one answer:* I don't know.

The tears flow down Héloïse's cheeks. Once more she sees
the book with its pink blotting-paper cover – in his beloved

hand. She hears Lawrence's oval voice saying: '*Je ne sais pas*'; the sad voice then repeat in English: 'I do not know'. The storm-whitened sea spitting at their hotel's window-panes. Lawrence had held her tight, kissed her forehead, the golden mane, without a word, struck dumb with love and melancholy. Héloïse herself is sure: she does not know. The meaning of her photos. The meaning of life. And their love.

'I write to him every day, like when I was small.'

'Did you write to him when you were small?'

'Love letters! I would take a stamp from your handbag and post the letters outside school.'

'Behind my back?'

'*Maman*, it was under your nose.'

'Did he reply?'

'Sometimes. When you invited him to dinner and he came up to say goodnight to me . . .'

'Lawrence went up to say goodnight to you?'

'Always. Have you forgotten?'

'Yes.'

'I was six . . . He read me stories . . . He would put English words in instead of French words, to annoy me . . . I loved his voice . . . his lips . . . I begged him to kiss me on the mouth . . .'

'What? Héloïse!'

'I was in love with him! Of course I wanted him to kiss me . . . I wanted him to do worse than that but I didn't dare ask . . .'

'You didn't even know that "worse than that" existed!'

'I guessed it did . . .'

'And how did he reply to your love letters?'

'Once he wrote back on a prescription: "Héloïse, obviously I accept your marriage proposal. However, I have no great desire to be married at your pony club, as you so kindly suggest. I would suggest, rather, the beach in Corsica, at the end of your grandmother's garden. With loving kisses to my little lion."'

'Tell me it's not true! With loving kisses to my six-year-old daughter!'

'That's nothing compared to what I was suggesting in my letters . . .'

Mirabelle's eyes become lost in thought. Héloïse observes her mother, who no longer dyes her hair, nor uses eyeshadow nor plucks her eyebrows. If no one is visiting, she will wear her Mickey Mouse slippers and her fleece dressing gown until it's time for her empty bed.

'Doesn't he reply to your letters?'

'Never.'

'What do you say in your letters?'

'That I've loved him since I was born! That I can wait another hundred years for him!'

'Don't cry, my darling . . .'

'He doesn't read them.'

'You don't know . . . Perhaps he does read them . . . Where are you writing to him? Rue des Martyrs?'

'Stop. He's gone back to rue de Rivoli.'

'Did Krishna tell you that?'

'Of course it was Krishna who told me. He spends half his time there!'

'I wanted to tell you but Lawrence asked me . . . You

know, I hate being the go-between . . . In any case, it's very recent . . .'

'It's been six months!'

'Héloïse . . . you have to be realistic . . . Lawrence is about to turn seventy! You are so . . . You're no comfort to him – with your youth and your beauty. Fleur is the same generation as him; it's simpler . . . They take care of their grandchildren . . . They have the same concerns . . . they're growing old together . . .'

'Growing old. It's meaningless.'

'It isn't, Héloïse. Trust me. It does mean something.'

The cello reaches them through the wall and throbs slowly. A long moment goes by. Night has fallen.

'Are you in love with *papa*?'

'No. Not the least bit.'

'Not even at first? When you met him?'

'I think he might have been in love with me. But he was never thoughtful . . . which suited me because I wanted a false partner. I was just after a stand-in, so I could forget Lawrence.'

'Did it work?'

'No, because Lawrence was everywhere. Your grandmother invited him to lunch at rue du Pas-de-la-Mule every Sunday. He'd come to Sciroccu every summer. At first he came alone . . . then with Fleur, whom he'd found at the Opéra . . . He had gone to pick her up as she left her dressing room. In the middle of lunch they used to describe how they met, laughing and kissing, right there in front of us . . . One year, Fleur showed up pregnant and I choked on a Barbary fig. The summers after that there were Fleur, Marine and

Justine . . . the three of them in their swimsuits on my jetty . . . the jetty of my childhood . . . When Marine and Justine were about ten, Lawrence had that episode with Violette . . . That went on for a few months . . . just when I was pregnant with you . . . Funny coincidence . . . He couldn't stand the thought of my having a child with Baptiste . . . with a musician . . . He had always dreamed of being an opera singer . . . And then Violette fell pregnant and *maman* was literally waiting on her hand and foot . . . She spent the whole time telling her to rest . . . and telling me: "You're forty years old, I hope it won't be a Down's child . . ." After three months, Violette got it into her head that Lawrence was the baby's father, when he wasn't . . . the dates didn't work . . . She knew that but she managed to forget . . . She hassled Lawrence . . . She threatened to tell Fleur everything – as if Fleur, poor thing, hadn't noticed what kind of a man she'd been living with for the past fifteen years . . . Violette called Lawrence on the night of the birth. She begged him to go with her to the hospital. He went, but only for half of it . . . He ran off just when the baby was about to come . . . Violette passed out . . . emergency Caesarian . . . They almost copped it the pair of them, Violette and Barnabé . . . I thought that would be the end of the story. But no . . . you and him.'

Both Héloïse and Mirabelle swallow, audibly.

'I knew it would end up like this. I could have sworn it would. It's as if I gave birth to you so that Lawrence would fall in love with you.'

There is a short silence so dense they can feel it.

'*Maman*, I know you were pregnant with his baby.'

'I miscarried.'

'I know . . . In the third month.'

'No, it was in the fourth month.'

'Were you very miserable?'

'What would I have done with a baby? I was twenty years old . . .'

'I was eighteen when I had Krishna.'

'That's too young.'

'Do you never think of it at all?'

'I do. I've always wondered how my life would have turned out . . . I was sorry.'

'Sorry about what?'

'Nothing! What has Lawrence told you?'

'Nothing . . . The same as you. That you had a miscarriage.'

1958. Mirabelle steps out of the 2CV parked outside the house on rue des Saints-Pères. She doesn't slam the door. She closes it softly. She bends down and, through the lowered window, says to Lawrence: no, he mustn't persist, she won't change her mind. Lawrence puts his hands on the wheel. Strange ideas appear in his fuggy head. He proposes to Mirabelle that they go for dinner on rue du Dragon that evening, to talk it all through. Mirabelle feels his panic throw itself, like an ape, at her fierce dress. The vile heat of its fur. Thirty-five degrees in the shade. The carnelian red bodywork of the car is boiling in the sun. Mirabelle is icy. She refuses the invitation to dinner. She has already made her decision, unshakeable though fragile. She would grow big alone, give birth alone, raise alone the baby they had begun together in the attic bedroom, up on the top floor. Lawrence looks into the rear-view mirror. The street is empty. The Leatherette seats are sweating. 'Come in, I want to kiss you.' Mirabelle sees the rue des Saints-Pères begin to warp, the asphalt to undulate weirdly. Shiny little puddles appear in the distance, like those on the smooth, slate-grey motorways that cut across the deserts of the western United States. Mirabelle opens the door and sits down. 'Get in the back with me.' Mirabelle finds herself on the back seat with no memory of making the slightest movement. A woman hastens along the pavement. She is escaping from the sun. Lawrence watches her move away. Buttocks squeezed inside her black polka-dot dress. Sunday: the hour that lazy lunches come to an end, dirty tablecloths, scattered with crumbs, stained with sauce and red wine. What is she doing, alone in the street? The woman turns right onto boulevard Saint-Germain. Mirabelle leans her face in close to Lawrence's. He puts one hand on her red mouth and the other on the white neck which he chokes with his fingers. The back of Mirabelle's head hits the window. She has enormous mad eyes, black, dashed with green, in which flicker light and tears. 'If you have this baby, I'll murder you.' His Irish accent.

XVII

'You look as though someone's died.'

'That's the idea.'

'Haven't you anything more cheery? Why don't you wear your tie with the canaries?'

'Héloïse . . . It's the custom. Is that what you're wearing today?'

'Pretty, isn't it?'

'Just once in your life . . .'

'What?'

'Be like everyone else. Take off that dress covered with sunflowers . . .'

'You think I'm about to change my dress?'

'My lion . . . It doesn't make any sense to you, fine. But for your family . . .'

'Wearing black to a funeral? On the contrary, that has a very particular meaning for me. It is about pissing with fear when you're confronted with death.'

'My Héloïse . . .'

'What, *my* Héloïse?'

'I adore you.'

'Then put something else on. Put on the canaries.'

'No. I'm going in black, like everyone else. Like an idiot.'

'That's not what I said.'

'But I said it. I agree with you. I would prefer death to be like your dress.'

'Have you ever fucked her?'

'Who?'

'Her, the reason for the funeral.'

Lawrence holds Héloïse's mouth in his. The cherry-red lipstick that she wore in Corsica; she was thirteen, lying out on the jetty, her foot pale and delicate, red nails in the sparkling wavelets. The chill waterfall taste of her kisses. Lawrence runs his hand through the long aromatic hair, July's shampoo. Héloïse lets her dress drop to the floor.

'Would you like to wank between my breasts?'

'No, I'd like to get to the funeral on time.'

'Then make yourself come fast.'

'I'm slow, you know me.'

'When was your last *branlette espagnole*?'

'A hundred years ago. Do you know how we say that in English?'

'Spanish wank?'

'French fuck.'

'Really?'

'Yes really, my little Frenchie.'

'Then I should say: Do you want a French fuck, Lawrence?'

Lawrence is sitting astride Héloïse, his penis between her breasts. He is still wearing his grey shirt and black suit jacket. One morning, he had come back. A Thursday of hail; their diamonds were puncturing umbrellas. Lawrence and Krishna had taken refuge in the recess of a coachhouse doorway. Hosts of frozen grasshoppers whipped at their calves, making giant leaps over the cars' bodywork. Since Héloïse and Lawrence had separated, Mirabelle had gone to pick Krishna up from his father and take him to Héloïse every Thursday. On Sundays, she had done the route in reverse, taking Krishna back to Lawrence, at the rue de Rivoli apartment. Héloïse and Lawrence never met. That morning of hail, Héloïse had opened the door with the same swift and joyous movement that she repeated every Thursday to welcome Krishna back. She was wearing a long T-shirt with the words Brown & Minkowski across it in flaky black letters. A souvenir from her last night in Boston with Vadim. Slipped on that morning of the attacks. Héloïse had never seen Vadim again. He had sent her text messages, those vibrating intruders in contemporary love. First he had sent messages of love.

It's crazy. I've never been so
happy. I want to spend
my life with you.

Pornographic messages.

I'm going to fuck you while
you lap at a bowl of milk
on all fours in my
kitchen.

Worried messages.

Are you frightened?
You can tell me everything,
my love.

Messages of supplication.

The only thing I ask of you
is to see me for 10 min. in
a café.
Say OK and I'll take the plane
to NY.

Bitter messages.

I found your photos
uninteresting.

The scent of Vadim, his caramel and ground-coffee skin, had long ago faded out of the Brown & Minkowski T-shirt. Héloïse would have preferred Lawrence to see her wearing something else. Her first words:

'Would it have put your cock out of joint to reply to one or two of my letters, you bastard?'

Two months later, Lawrence and Héloïse were moving into a loft in the 11th *arrondissement*, near the Père Lachaise cemetery. A glass cylinder, greenery and steel. A giant banana palm in the living room and, beneath its long fanned-out leaves,

Héloïse's black panther, its stuffed snarl. Bathtub of black volcanic rock in the bay window. Mirabelle found it 'anonymous and chilly'; Jeanne 'very spacious'; Violette 'divine'; Krishna 'sick and mega cool'.

Little by little, Lawrence introduces his penis between the squeezed breasts.
　'You're squashing my belly.'
　'It was your idea, French girl . . .'
　'You're not going about it right, my love . . .'
　'It would work better with bigger breasts.'
　'Or a bigger cock.'
　'My lion . . .'
　'What?'
　'Are we going to the funeral?'
　'Tell me first. Have you fucked Jeanne?'
　'Scarlett . . . in your position I'd be ashamed to ask such a question . . . on a day like today . . .'
　'I would be ashamed to have fucked someone's daughter, mother, aunt and grandmother.'

They are all in black; they are all too hot. Except for Héloïse, in her sunflowers. And Violette, in pink polka dots. The sun shines on the long hearse. Mirabelle presses her nose to the smoked glass. Her mother's coffin. Someone from the funeral parlour has left behind the wrapper from his Big Mac on the front seat. The coffin seems too big. Jeanne was not tall. One metre fifty-eight. There must be some space between Jeanne and the oak sides. Mirabelle hears Héloïse's voice. She turns around, sees her. Her joyful body, and Lawrence, his arm around her waist. Mirabelle remembers the clinic in Geneva. The long tunic with buttons down the back that the nurse had asked her to put on in a strangely gentle voice, avoiding her eye, as if she were trying not to see Mirabelle, her twenty years, her fingers' frightful clasping and unclasping. The doctor had a fine blonde moustache. The foetus, a dirty little swarm of red and grey, had emerged noisily. 'It is very large, mademoiselle. In my opinion, you were a good deal further on than fourteen weeks.' There had been a 'complication'. Mirabelle thought she was dying. Haemorrhage, with two 'h's and two 'r's.

Héloïse takes Mirabelle's hand. The coffin inside the undertaker's car. The car in the street. The street where other people go by, brush past them, full of energy. At the age of ninety-eight, Jeanne has died in a young girl's accident. Waking in the middle of the night, she drags a wicker chair up against the wardrobe. Climbs onto it. Reaches right to the back, for the shoebox lurking in the dust. The tip of her middle finger upon the lid, she gently slides the box out. Her feet rip through the cane weave of the seat. She falls. Screams. Head against the sharp bedpost. Blood. Death, and the soul's exit up the chimney. The box of secrets – letters, dried flowers, yellowed photographs, pendants and other lovers' trinkets – comes down on Jeanne's already broken head. The cigarette case she was after lands on her heart. Jeanne's last thought: 'Darn! The photo!'

Sciroccu, 1989. The storm brings its lightning bolt down on the oldest and tallest pine in the garden. The howling flames thrash among the branches and swell their foliage. A hot air balloon of fire; the black sea pricked with foamy white storm-tossed drops. Scent of rain and burnt wood. Jeanne, Mirabelle, Violette, Héloïse, Barnabé, Lawrence, Fleur, Marine, Justine and Ange, the gardener, dishevelled in the rain, eyes fixed on the magical pyre. The partly cut cake drowns on the table. They are celebrating Héloïse's twelfth birthday. Milky custard moustache along her top lip. Her soaked white blouse. Lawrence's gaze steers from the flames to the childish breasts. *As long as one day, drop by drop, Héloïse's sex drains into my mouth. As long as my hands encircle her waist. As long as my tongue dips into her arse.* Jeanne says they must call the fire brigade. The rain and the tree's crackling drown out her voice. She motions to Lawrence to follow her. They go back past the lunch table – glasses knocked over, cake and custard diluted by the rain – around the corner of the house and in through the pantry. Their clinging, waterlogged clothes leave puddles on the red tiles. Jeanne kneels. She undoes Lawrence's belt-buckle.

'Let me . . .'

'Get up.'

'You've liked me . . . for thirty years! Now – what? Am I too old?'

'The garden's on fire.'

'You disgust me, Lawrence!'

'Don't shout . . . Stand up.'

'Do not give me orders! I was here before the others! Before Fleur! Before Violette! I've lasted longer than all your other women! You need me, Lawrence!'

'I'm going to call the firemen. Pour yourself a glass of wine.'

'This is my house! I'll have wine or I'll not have it! You are here at my request! I am not one of your tarts! I do not toast the health of tarts!'

'Jeanne, that's enough.'

'I've had Dodo and I've had you in my life. Two egotists. You think you're powerful but you're pathetic. You don't love anyone.'

'I agree with you.'

'You have told no one except me about your father! His rages! I'm the only one who knows your childhood terrors! The curtains! The vast curtains full of ghosts – who knows about them beside me?'

'Jeanne, we're not talking about the same things.'

'And don't imagine that time has forgotten you! You're not thirty any more either!'

'I'm not attracted to you any longer, Jeanne.'

'You wept in my arms when Fleur left to stay with her mother in Châtellerault for a month because she couldn't bear it with you another second! When Violette fell pregnant and wanted to make you take the rap! You wept in my arms! These are the same arms!'

'I remember very well.'

'That isn't enough!'

'I am grateful for everything you have done for me.'

'You are the most ungrateful creature I know!'

'My God, Jeanne! You want to suck my cock? You want me to grit my teeth? You want me to close my eyes so as not to see how old you are?'

'You can't hurt me any longer. Everything hurts.'

'What can I say to you?'

'You used to find plenty to say to me, didn't you? Right

here! On this table! While Mirabelle was waiting for you on the beach!'

'I'm asking you a question. What can I say to you now?'

'Tell me you love me a little!'

'Do you hear what you're saying? Come . . . stay proud.'

'Proud! Thanks to you, I have felt old and grotty since the age of thirty! And I've no idea why I let that happen . . . I could have built a new life after Dodo; I was still pretty . . . I want a souvenir. Give me a present, Lawrence.'

Lawrence takes a black cigarette case with an embossed silver shamrock from his pocket and places it in Jeanne's pathetically extended hand. In thirty years, the pantry has not changed: the smell of damp earth, of basil, the raw pine shelves, the neat ranks of jars, the humming of the fridge, the ham dangling from its hook, the table where Lawrence had taken Jeanne from behind, that first time, her dress pulled up over her hips, white underpants held aside with his fingers, the port-wine stain at the base of her back. He was nineteen. Jeanne was the mother of his girlfriend, his unripe Mirabelle; Jeanne was a woman. His very audacity was intoxicating. He gripped the brown and grey plait in his fist and into the delicate ear, set with a pearl, he whispered filthy things that rose up into his head like fine spirits, or fury.

There are five firemen. The storm has put out the fire. The scorched branches are smoking, raised against a torn sky, half of it a deep, dark blue. Jeanne grips the cigarette case in her mauve-veined hand. The fire chief, all chrome and gold, looks out over the paths lined with oleanders and Barbary figs leading into the sea. 'It's truly a beautiful property you have here!' Jeanne weeps and does not wipe away her tears. 'I understand your distress, madam, but it's just a tree! You can plant another! Just think: it could have struck your house instead!'

At the beginning of the sixties, Laoghaire Calvagh, professor of linguistics at Trinity College Dublin, had presented Lawrence with a cigarette case set with a shamrock. 'I bought it for your mother's birthday but, with her tuberculosis, it would be terribly poor taste.' The cigarette case is the only present Lawrence ever received from his father. His mother, Margareth Calvagh, reigned over the world of presents. She chose them, she arranged them by the birthday cake, she smiled with pleasure when Lawrence tore off the paper, untied the ribbons. Lawrence noticed that his father always discovered what the parcels contained at the same moment that he did, and he was hurt. 'The shamrock, my son, is so that you never forget where you come from, your homeland.' Mr Calvagh was an obstinate, erudite man, a hater of tea, the English accent, Shakespeare and George VI. To be precise, he detested the English. Hence he did his best not to broadcast his passion for T. E. Lawrence, also known as Lawrence of Arabia. In adoration of the greatest British spy of all time, Laoghaire chose this name for his son. By way of education, he had pursued a unique and strenuous programme: making Lawrence ingest the complete works of Jonathan Swift, Bram Stoker, George Moore, James Joyce, Oscar Wilde, George Bernard Shaw and W. B. Yeats. Lawrence spent the Sundays of his childhood shut away in his father's great wood-panelled study, with its smells of wax and damp, the vast volume of *Ulysses* open on his lap. To stop

Lawrence from rejoicing at every circuit completed by the hour hand, Laoghaire covered the clock with brown tartan. The torture of time that does not pass. And in order that Lawrence not be distracted by the dance of humanity and the pools of light mirrored up from Dublin's rainy streets, Laoghaire would draw the curtains. Two endless, green velvet curtains that held ghosts and shifted about with their torment. Mr Calvagh's pedagogic methods inspired in his son a taste for escape and a fierce, incurable hatred of Irish literature.

The sun enters through one stained glass window, *The Agony in the Garden of Olives,* and throws pink and blue lozenges over the coffin in the central aisle. Mirabelle holds Violette's hand. In the second row, an old woman turns to her daughter:

'It seems that when they found her body, she was clasping a cigarette case to her chest . . . You'll never guess what was inside it . . .'

'What? Don't talk so loud.'

'A photo of Lawrence Calvagh!'

'Shush, *maman!*'

'But wait . . . a photo of Lawrence Calvagh . . . naked as the day he was born!'

'That's gossip.'

'And look what he's done to that young Herschel girl! Dreadful!'

'She's not so young. She's thirty-five.'

'And he dares to show his face in God's house . . .'

'Shut up, *maman!*'

'That man is the devil incarnate.'

The most important event of the ceremony was the punch. They were leaving the church, walking down the aisle, when a fist caught Lawrence on the chin as he stood there, equidistant between Jeanne's coffin and Héloïse's big belly, six months pregnant with a pair of twins.

XVIII

BARNABÉ'S STORY

Barnabé is one month old. Héloïse is there.

Barnabé is seven. Héloïse is his delight, his mother superior, his cellmate in Alcatraz, all the faces of their made-up worlds.

Barnabé is fourteen. Héloïse is the erection, the only sex of the other sex.

Barnabé is fifteen. Héloïse is the pain, the vile desire, another man's pleasure.

Barnabé is nineteen. Héloïse is a mother, transatlantic, a golden skyscraper and milk.

Barnabé is twenty-five. Fanny has something of Héloïse about her.

Barnabé is twenty-seven. Fanny is wearing a swan-white dress and Héloïse kisses the newly-weds' pink cheeks.

Barnabé is thirty-five. His fist strikes Lawrence's chin at top speed, between the coffin in its blue and pink light and Héloïse's belly.

Barnabé is thirty-seven. Fanny takes the photo albums, little Marie-Anne and slams the door as she leaves.

Barnabé is forty-nine. He votes, in the referendum, in favour of bringing back capital punishment. Héloïse despises him.

Barnabé is ninety-nine. He dies in a bedroom in Sciroccu, on the goat side of the house. Héloïse keeps his vigil.

XIX

An unexpected and happy event, caused by a protozoic parasite, occurred in Krishna's seventeenth year. For almost a month the birds had been dying of diarrhoea by the dozen. They were found all over Central Park, lying stiff or paddling shakily in the green mulch of their last evacuations. Dressed in white overalls with fluorescent bands, representatives of New York City's sanitation authorities took samples from the park's seven water features. An alarmist article in the *New York Times* revealed that this fatal gastroenteritis was due to a high concentration of *Cryptosporidium parvum* in the Turtle Pond. Carefully packed away in fifty tubs of water, the turtles were carried by lorries to the Bronx Zoo. As if for a crime scene, yellow and black plastic tape ran from tree to tree around the Turtle Pond, encircling the fluorescent men and their slow, chemical movements, their faces muzzled with fearful filter masks. After eight hours of pumping, a great gurgling was heard, a stomach, the sound of a belch: the pond was empty. Two greedy tubes sucked at the muddy bottom, strewn with an infinite number of objects buried in the sludge. The crowd behind the tape was observing and photographing the begloved lunar gentlemen as they passed the treasures of the deeps from hand to hand and laid them out on a vast tarpaulin:

a crack pipe made from a water bottle pierced with a Bic ballpoint; a VHS cassette of *Jaws*; a factor thirty sunscreen spray; a French translation of Nabokov's *Lolita*; hundreds of quarters stamped with George Washington's profile and the bald eagle; a white Apple Mac mouse; two cases of condoms, Durex King Size and Manix Regular; a Sony Walkman; bent stripy red-and-white straws; a small model spaceship; Coca-Cola Light, Pepsi, Dr Pepper, Cherry Coke and root beer cans; pairs of sunglasses; a sledge; a plastic Superman; rusty beer and soda caps that formed a colony of shells at the bottom of the pond; a gigantic Telefunken TV set; a red lipstick; a Goodyear tyre; a four-wheeled rollerskate; a Singer sewing machine, the manufacture date, 1958, engraved on the steel throat plate; an Energizer lithium battery; a breast implant that was at first thought to be a jellyfish; a complete blister pack of contraceptive pills and a pack of Trizivir – medication prescribed in the treatment of HIV – its bubbles empty and punctured; a quartz watch; Sophie the giraffe, who squeaked between the fingers of a sanitation security agent; a broken bottle of Malibu; a car GPS system; a hula hoop; a diary that locked with a key; a Game Boy console with a Tetris game inserted; an orange Bic razor; a wooden skateboard; a red aerosol paint canister; a 512 MB USB stick; a pair of glasses with wide black frames, fashionable in the 1950s and in 2010; plastic discs that had once graced cups of Fanta, Sprite and Coca-Cola; a standard camera; a flick-knife; baseballs; a pack of Lucky Strike with the words 'Smoking can kill' on it in a black rectangle; a *South Park* keyring; the shells of dead turtles; a baby's bottle; a Barbie doll in a swimsuit; a vibrator shaped like a dolphin; mobile phones; a school rucksack that had belonged to Cody Richardson and had been thrown into the Turtle Pond deliverately by Kyle Coen who had caught his girlfriend Consuela kissing Cody with tongues in the Documentation and Information Centre of St Bernard High School; a wedding ring on which could be read, engraved in the gold, 'Emily and Bentley forever'; the discoloured rags of Mars, Kit Kat and Twix wrappers; a steel box padlocked shut; a PVC crucifix with the words 'JESUS LOVES YOU!' around its pink base; a dental brace made up of a cherry-red palate and a rusty metal arch; two Converse trainers, their laces knotted together; shuttlecocks; syringes; an MP3 player; an infant's pram with articulated sunshade; a cassette player from the 1970s; a wooden crocodile, faintly green, trailing a leash from its neck.

Justine let out an explosive 'FUCK!' In her kitchen in Brooklyn, threw the *New York Times* down on the table where baby macaroni and streaks of ketchup vied for space on the wipeclean cloth that was perforated with cigarette-stub craters, and insulted her phone, which shook in her hands.

'Fuck! Koko's in the papers! They found him!'

'Is that you, Justine?'

'Oh shit, sweetheart . . . What time is it over there?'

'It's four o'clock . . .'

'In the morning? Those fuckers have drained the Turtle Pond in Central Park and picked up Koko! Krishna's crocodile! You remember how he screamed?'

'They fished up Koko?'

'He's in the photo! A close-up in the *New York Times*! They've found millions of old bits and pieces! Even fifteen kilos of cocaine padlocked into a steel box! That's about 500,000 dollars' worth of coke . . . It was a secret drop . . . They put the charlie inside, left the cache in where it wasn't too deep and when—'

'Hang on, Justine . . . I'm coming over with the twins.'

'To New York?'

Héloïse had never seen anything like it; never touched such solid poetry. Beneath the glass dome of the Olympic stadium in Queens, the thousands of objects fished out of the mud of the Turtle Pond made up a three-dimensional tableau of twentieth-century American history. The automobile, industrialisation, television, the conquest of outer space, fashion, rock music, sexual liberation, drugs, computing, evangelism, fast food, AIDs and cosmetic surgery. The items had effectively been arranged in squares to form aisles that crossed at right angles. The extensive grid recalled the geometric vision of the New World's pioneers, the rectilinear shaping of the States and the cities with their long perpendicular streets. Héloïse crouched down in the centre of this American territory. She hesitated to reach out to him, as if Koko were still alive. She stroked the wooden scales, tears springing to her eyes, the memory kicked forward into the present by the green scales, eroded by water after the thousand touches of Krishna's fingers. The obese council worker, who had extraordinarily long, curved, petrol-blue fake nails, pulled a paper tissue from her pocket and waved it like a bell in front of Héloïse, who smiled, chagrined, apparently by way of apology for weeping over a children's toy. The council worker laughed with unexpected goodwill, which only made Héloïse cry harder.

'*Maman*? Why are you sad?'

The voice was layered. A child's voice that bore its own echo. On the first step of the terraces that rose steeply towards the glass dome were sitting, side by side and implausibly blonde, Margaux and Juliette, the three-year-old twins.

'It's nothing, my little chickadees . . . *Maman* is crying because she has found a crocodile.'

Héloïse secured authorisation from New York's mayoress to make use of the 'Turtle Pond collection' in creating a photographic artwork of her own choosing, on condition that it illustrate the social and cultural history of New York, which was to say: of the entire United States, and indeed of the whole planet. First of all, Justine and Héloïse had meticulously and interminably photographed and numbered the 3,769 objects found in the pond. They had then inundated the local press with photos and detailed descriptions. They were extending an invitation to anyone convinced they had owned one of these trifling treasures, mutilated by water and the passage of time, to come and identify themselves beneath that Olympic dome. In exchange for the travel costs and time spent, they were offering five dollars' compensation. There followed talented fantasists, amnesiac pensioners and a few, very few, genuine owners. But all, sat there on the terrace steps, did their best to reply accurately to the questions of Héloïse and Justine, who wrote up the tales, word by word, on the laptops they were balancing on their knees. The exhibition was called *The History of the Greatest World Power of All Time, Greater Even than Babylon, Rome and the Mongol Empire of Genghis Khan* and it was an unqualified success. It toured the world.

Krishna was able to admire his crocodile near the Paris Trocadéro, on the walls of the Palais de Tokyo gallery. Koko appeared in several posters, accompanied now by condom packs and the Trizivir blister strip, now by the spaceship, now the crucifix and now the lipstick – which had been used to write along his tail: PUNK IS NOT DEAD. Beside each photo there was a quotation from a liar or legitimate owner.

It was with this sewing machine, no kidding, that my wife Beth hemmed the pants I was wearing in the crowd when Kennedy took that bullet in the nut. (Mike O'Ridge, 83)

These fucking coins are mine and no one else's! I was throwing one in every day so that Daisy would come home . . . like when you light a candle, see . . . She never came back! Exit Daisy (Stage Left)! So if it's no trouble to you, miss, I'll just reclaim my savings! (Jimmy Bates, 54)

I swear, man, it's my pack of rubbers! I always use King Size! I can still see meself screwing Michelle next to the pond . . . You could hear the frogs . . . She was going: 'Oh no Jacky! Oh no Jacky! What if somebody sees us!' (Jacky Garland, 21)

In the Fake Gallery in San Francisco, 8,954 kilometres from the Palais de Tokyo, Katharine Szalowski gave a yelp on discovering, on Koko's back, the 'Big Red One', insignia of America's Ist Infantry Division, which her father had been wearing on his shoulder when he was fatally wounded by a shell-burst in Picardy, on 6 November 1918. Hunched over in the wheel-chair her great-granddaughter Meadow was pushing, Katherine murmured: 'Thank you.' She died a few weeks later aged a hundred and five, not even of the flu; of nothing, of having completed her life. On the same day, Héloïse celebrated her fortieth birthday surrounded by her family, except for her aunt Violette who had twice defeated the killer crab but succumbed the third time.

Héloïse holds her father by the arm and guides him from one photo to the next, showing him where to look by pointing out the details herself: the brown-and-red rust on a Cherry Coke can, the remarkable tightness of the knotted shoelace that ties the Converse trainers together . . .

'Don't think I've never been interested in your photos . . . I've seen all your exhibitions.'

'Perhaps not all of them . . .'

'Every one! But I must say I often . . . especially at first . . . Anyway, this one, in any case, is a very fine show.'

'*Papa*, what did you mean to say?'

'Well, you see . . . for example . . . I didn't like that series with the ovens. You were very young, but that idea of making fun of ovens, with your homosexual model in a stripy suit . . . I don't think there's art to be made on the back of that.'

'"That" – "those" are the concentration camps!'

'Concentration camps! You were born thirty years after the war! Thanks be to God, you have no idea what you're talking about.'

'You think the camps belong to you because your parents died in them?'

Baptiste drops Héloïse's arm. They have stopped in front of a spectacularly magnified blister-strip of contraceptive pills.

'Are you crazy? What's got into you?'

'Art and life – they're the same. There's art to be made on the back of everything.'

'Your mother isn't Jewish, so you're not Jewish! That's how it is! You can look at it any way you like and it won't make a blind bit of difference!'

'What has that to do with what I said? Must someone be Jewish to say the word "Jew"? I say that art can be about a genocide as much as it can be about a kernel of sweetcorn or a pair of balls.'

'And I believe that art should be about the finer sentiments! For the beauty of the world! Art should try to do good, whereas you . . . your photos are hostile! They're violent! And I'm not the only one who thinks so . . . I've read a few reviews . . . Don't you read the reviews?'

Héloïse holds back the words that have been growing inside her for a good long time. Baptiste strokes his cheeks, shaved two hours earlier, still pink from the scraping of the triple blade, smelling of his soothing aftershave.

'Héloïse, you don't have to agree with me. I'm telling you how I see it, that's all.'

Héloïse glares straight into her father's forget-me-not blue eyes, soon defused by rapid blinking.

'Art can be about everything. Even about bruises.'

And it was as if that word, 'bruises', exploded out of Héloïse's mouth, dynamiting the entrance to a cave, and all the light and air of the spring, laden with salt and the pistils of flowers, sank into its depths.

'Bruises?'

'Yes, *papa* . . . the purple marks. Blood that's coagulated under the skin. When you hit . . . it's not like hitting the water in a lake . . . It leaves marks.'

Multi-coloured lozenges, some kind of sweetie, microbes blown up under the microscope, dance before Baptiste's eyes. He rests a hand on the giant strip of contraceptive pills. Through the haze of psychedelic cells, he can make out the polished tips of his shoes, irreproachable, as if brand new.

XX

Mirabelle is ready. Sitting there, she taps the top of her head –
not a strand has come free of the clip. The handbag on her
knees and the iridescent scarab sheen of her new skirt. The
silence of the clean, dry, well-ordered apartment. A single lamp
lit, a dolly for its shade. Footsteps, outside, in the stairwell.
Mirabelle raises a finger to silence an invisible friend. The steps
on the other side of the door, the weary, regular sound of
unerotic low heels. Madame Murciélago probably. Mirabelle
sighs, scratches at the embossed downstrokes and upstrokes
of the invitation card. She thinks again of the wedding ceremony on the little beach at Sciroccu. Héloïse was wearing
a long dress of red tussah silk, Lawrence a very tall, old-
fashioned grey topper. Barefoot, both of them. Rice was
thrown over the newly-weds. People laughed at their romantic
obstinacy, at this shameless love that had, without apology,
thrashed every other heart round about. A toast was drunk
to the victory of the selfish lovers. Joy held the family in its
palm. Marine smiled, her arm linked with Fleur's. Faded Fleur
with her beautiful, sweetly sorrowful eyes. Fuchsia-hued petals
of bougainvillea were thrown as high as they would go, and
whole handfuls of rice tossed out into the sea and sky were
transfixed by camera flashes, then fell back upon the top hat,

the red silk veil and the sand – complicit since that first erotic hour. Jeanne was watching the ceremony, her ghost of lace. *I thought I saw her take a cigarette out of the black case with its silver shamrock stamp, saw her standing on the stump of the old pine. The one that had been struck by lightning in that other life when we were all young, whatever our age. All in love. And in return, Lawrence loved us all, at times.*

The priest was wearing sports socks with his sandals. Héloïse had plucked him from the mountains, on the winding Corte road. She had parked in front of the church of St Mary of the Assumption, her candy-pink Citroën Méhari hypnotising the cows resting on the bends in the road. From the church square you could see the receding planes of the mountains, the graduations of blue from the sky into the sea. Héloïse took Father Daniel by the arm and led him to the sacristy where a Virgin and Child, eroded by prayer, had been stored away. The child had been beheaded. A thief: mad or a prankster. Héloïse pointed to the base of the severed neck. The absent head was there – in the mind of the beholder – the immanent template of little Jesus: the rounded forehead, the determined little mouth, the cheeks swollen with health, the oval outline of the chin. And the legs frozen mid-movement, sculpted pedalling for joy, as babies do in their first months of life. Héloïse said to the priest that she had loved Lawrence since she was born. That he was losing his memory. That she still did not know who he was. That, oddly, it was time for them to be married. Father Daniel nodded, surprised by the naivety and loving determination of this very young girl of fifty. Héloïse went on to specify that she was a little Jewish by her father's line and very slightly Catholic thanks to her mother. She spent the night with the priest, talking about their love affairs until the moon dropped from the sky. Each to his own. Lawrence Calvagh and Jesus of Nazareth. In the small hours, they climbed into the open-topped Méhari and took to the road, amid skies of showy pink, all the way to Sciroccu. Upon the terrace, lying on his chaise longue, the fiancé. An old man astonished at this last stunt she was trying on him. Lawrence was tanned, thin, elegant; his loose bow tie blew about in the breeze. A top hat awaited the great occasion on a garden table.

Father Daniel shook Lawrence's hand and, without malice, asked him the secret of his youthfulness.

'Olive oil.'

Héloïse replied for her fiancé. She did not like compliments.

It was Héloïse's idea.

'Marry me.'

'You hate weddings.'

'On the beach in Sciroccu.'

'In that case . . . I'll think about it.'

'If you think about it, I'll murder you.'

'How could you do it, Scarlett, murder an old man who is half-mad already?'

'I would murder you with pleasure, Rhett . . . Orgasmic to send your head up in flames.'

Mirabelle's hands are tanned. She massages her thumb joints. *I love your old hands, like an old fairy.* She stayed in Sciroccu for a month after the wedding. Each corner of the house awakened ten long-lost memories. On a white stone path, blinding at midday, bathed in red gold at the day's end, she saw grandmother

Joséphine, with her wizardly ways, cutting sprays of sage and thyme with scissors. She saw her sister Violette with her butterfly net, lost for the last eighty years. She saw Jeanne and Ange drawing chalk crosses on the hackberry trees that were to be pruned. She scolded the children, Héloïse and Barnabé, who were torturing a lizard, channelling the blazing sun with a magnifying glass. Mirabelle closes her eyes, takes the stone staircase that carries on from the jetty, along the terrace, the plain canvas deckchairs, the eucalyptus trailing great rags of bark, the bushes of broom, the Cape and Barbary figs with their pantomime shapes. Up there, the house, and on the balcony, on tiptoes, Jeanne, her scarf in the wind, gazing at the distant pines dancing to their own jazz, the mahogany speedboat, the sea, waiting for someone to arrive or something to happen, among the blue and sparkling mirages of the summer, the seasonal regrets.

Mirabelle observes her hands, the fragile skin, the sunspots, the purple veins that race towards her heart. Justine told her: 'I love your old hands, like an old fairy' just as Héloïse and Lawrence were saying in front of everyone: 'I will be your wife,' 'I will be your husband.' Justine came from New York with a tall, thin, quiet girl she called 'my raccoon'. Marine, who was not expected to come, was sitting in the first row with her husband, her three children and her granddaughter Fleur, to whom, throughout her life, people would say: you have the name of your great-grandmother who was a brilliant dancer, who married Lawrence, you know, the Irishman, the doctor, the Don Juan, the one who wanted to be an opera singer and who, at an age when life offers nothing more, ran away with a child forty years younger than himself. Mirabelle has knitted a jacket for little Fleur. She knits badly but, as soon as a baby is born, her fingers itch for needles and a ball of wool. Mirabelle thinks it quite sad for a baby to be born without a knitted jacket that will fit for only a moment, a dazzling memory, a photograph, a spring afternoon, then will immediately be too small, a mirror to our fleeting lives, which leave behind them cases of clothes grown too small. Mirabelle doesn't understand time any longer. There was a time when time made its way slowly, at a regular pace. And here she is, very old, she, young Mirabelle who kissed fifteen-year-old Nassim at the top of Aïdour. She catches her reflection in a photograph on the wall. Aloud, she calls herself an old crone, giggles, and wipes some dust from the edge of the frame with the tip of her finger. A 60,000 dollar present from Héloïse. Mirabelle shrugs.

Each photo Héloïse takes is equal to twenty-five years of my salary at Artik. Yet I used to get up early. I took the metro, standing through four seasons of heat, full carriages, the bodies touching my nauseated body, the heavy vanilla scents, the bloody razor nicks on Adam's apples, open novels, seventeen irreconcilable, cacophonous stories read at the same time, in the same subterranean passage, the morning papers, 'SENSATIONAL!' on the cover of L'Equipe, the thick make-up, wavering lines of kohl, orangey foundation, shining skins, spots, whiteheads, coffee breath, suits, briefcases, the girls who bit their nails, the girls who found themselves in their reflections in the windows. I used to have lunch with my boss's secretary in a Japanese restaurant. Always the same. Miso soup. Cabbage salad with soy. Tuna and salmon kebabs. Red bean cake. Closed on Mondays. On Mondays I used to have a salad with lentils, mango, roasted pine nuts, white onions, feta and Thai basil that I prepared the night before, singing above the radio, old-fashioned songs. I could hear the sound of my own chewing. Swallowing. You hear yourself eating when you eat alone. I would dip my fork into a plastic bowl that I set up on my computer keyboard. The two kids at the office with their stupid stares used to feel sorry for me. In the first weeks, they suggested I come along to their yoga class, in the basement of a shopping centre adjoining the train station. Later they just waved to me with apologetic smiles. They were always getting new handbags and calling each other *ma belle*. The expression spread like an epidemic. After a few months, all the women at Artik were calling all the other women *ma belle*. The men caught it too, calling all the women *ma belle*, even those who least deserved it. I continued to use people's names. It wasn't much appreciated. I was not fashionable. All my life, I have dressed so as not to be hot in the summer nor cold in the winter. No more stylish than that. But I liked soft tops, the simple and luxurious feel of cashmere on my breasts – I have never worn a bra. Monsieur Varela, my boss in the shiny shirt, used to say: 'You have to be trendy in order to understand anything in advertising, because advertising is about what's happening now.' And I would stare at the pattern of his shirt and say nothing. I would smile wickedly in secret.

A 60,000 dollar present. A large photograph entitled *We Wanted a Girl* exhibited in New York and Los Angeles at the beginning of the new millennium. A father, mother and son paddling, their feet in scarlet water in which the tiny stars of jasmine blossom and miniature corpses are floating. Lawrence, the father, has white hair, a brown tweed suit, sunspots painted on his forehead, cheeks and neck. An expression of senile joy. Héloïse, the mother, is wearing a white T-shirt, a sparkling dental brace, a hygienic blonde ponytail; her legs are bare, a few auburn pubic hairs show beneath the T-shirt. She smiles but her eyes are two mirrors of perfectly balanced water, ready to pour. Héloïse and Lawrence each rest a hand on one of their son's shoulders: Krishna is fifteen in the photo. He has the beginning of a beard and is wearing a sea-blue velvet hairband, a pink dress with puffy sleeves, green eyeshadow, lipstick that has smudged a little onto his philtrum. In the glass of the photo Mirabelle observes her own lipstick fraying around her mouth. No one ever told her, when she was little, that one day her lips would be overrun by wrinkles along which would drain her every attempt at youth or femininity.

Héloïse had given her the photo at the family gathering at rue du Pas-de-la-Mule. The annual St Nicholas's Day holiday. The day when children are allowed to be naughty in the corners and when parents measure the passage of time. Mirabelle had felt proud. The present proved something. She no longer knows what. An impression. An unspoken understanding with Héloïse. The pride of having given birth, of being responsible for her life and for the art that flew from her brain. Being given the photo in front of everyone was an ennoblement, a maternal metamorphosis. Mirabelle was becoming an eccentric mother. They all paid their dues to the huge photograph which Mirabelle had unrolled on the table, next to the blinis with lumpfish roe. Héloïse enjoyed the reactions, the murmurs, the looks of revulsion, anger, delight, disgust, enthusiasm, astonishment, mockery: the full range of human emotions. Around the tree, everyone said their piece.

'She's mad.'

'So poetic!'

'She has a sense of humour.'

'She must be an unhappy person.'

'She has an eye for colour.'

'She's going to turn Krishna gay.'

'Boy, can she be unsavoury!'

'Mirabelle doesn't know how to handle it! She'll feel obliged to hang it in her bedroom . . . How dreadful when you're trying to sleep!'

After Jeanne's death, the family stopped coming together for St Nicholas's Day in the great drawing room of the apartment on rue du Pas-de-la-Mule. The apartment was sold to a Chinese businessman who hung drapes of crimson velvet on the walls, installed four-poster beds in all the rooms and replaced the eighteenth-century tiles with slabs of green marble. The apartment was split into five studio units and each one let for 1,500 euros a week to American and Chinese tourists, through the agency Paris Authenticité. Jeanne's furniture was shared among her sisters, her three nieces, her daughter Mirabelle and her grandchildren Barnabé and Héloïse. There were arguments. Each discovered a visceral attachment to whatever little footstool they stood not to inherit. Each felt they had lost a part of themselves when they caught sight of the pedestal table, which they had hidden under as a child, in the home of a cousin. Héloïse claimed the chaise longue with its Provençal upholstery, which Lawrence was attached to, and an old coffee grinder that reminded her of Jeanne, of the vigorous move-ment of her elbow as she turned the handle, seeming to expel in nervous jerks years of mute anger and of finely rendered thoughts, as bitter as the roasted beans she was grinding into powder. Before selling the apartment, Mirabelle had to sift through sixty years of daily life, a sediment of clothes, photo-graphs, trinkets so familiar that no one saw them any longer on the countless odd surplus pieces of furniture: a rosewood master chest-of-drawers, a Louis XV plant stand, a dough trough chest, a chiffonnier, the whole family of pedestal tables. In the writing desk's lockable drawer, Mirabelle found a personal diary that Jeanne had begun the day she was married and finished nineteen years later, the day Mirabelle's Baccalaureate results came out. The gaps were always followed by excuses: *I'm sorry, I've not written a word for three years and I don't know where to begin again.*

Mirabelle hesitated for a moment. But no more than a moment. The diary had only to hide what it was intended to hide. Sooner or later, it risked being read. Its author had to accept this risk of desecration, to weigh it up when opening her heart – and leave out those events or states of mind she could not admit. Basically, the author of a diary should write while constantly reminding herself that her egoistical work will one day be surrendered to an indiscreet posterity. A diary was like a kiss in the middle of the street: both intimate and public at once. Mirabelle was trembling from the very first lines. She had to read and reread to be sure she had read correctly. Her mother loved and admired her. Jeanne wrote of Violette as the more outgoing of the two sisters, the one overflowing with life, the more unusual. But it was to

Mirabelle that she devoted her longest passages, seeing in her qualities that she found lacking in herself: patience, warmth. Mirabelle remembered her mother wandering wildly in the long L-shaped corridor of their Marseille apartment, unable to see or hear anything, quite blinded by her suffering. On the contrary – she had seen everything. Her senses had been razor sharp. Not a week passed without her noting how sweetly Mirabelle watched over her sister, smiling at her tantrums, making up lullabies, planting kisses on the little cheeks flushed by teething. On 6 August 1950, Jeanne wrote: *Mirabelle's presence in this awful apartment is such a wonderful relief. I have nothing left. Without her I might do something stupid. I am brave and weary enough to know that I am not lying.*

Mirabelle would have liked to read these words when she was descending the steep slopes of adolescence. She would have faced adulthood with greater confidence, without brooding over her indolent and incomplete time as a student, without cursing the day she had been hired to work in an advertising agency, on the recommendation of a friend of Lawrence and because she lacked her own calling. Then the world would not have divided into two tribes: the passionate ones, like Violette with her horses, Baptiste with his cello, Lawrence with his hospital; and the rest, colourless, flat, unworthy of flourishing under the sun's extravagant rays.

In her diary, Jeanne wrote of Georges in a way that surprised Mirabelle. She did not criticise him – having nevertheless done so from dawn 'til dusk in Marseille, whining like a dog, tarot cards laid out on her desk. She did not hold him responsible for her unhappiness. She hardly reproached him for leaving her to live with Ouarda, *a poor child whom he will protect with the*

*authority of a father, whom he'll never know how to listen to and whom
he'll make suffer while thinking he's saving her life.* Jeanne wrote
that the primary cause of their discord had been that they
had not known how to make love. *We are getting it wrong, both
of us, in how we approach it; only I get it wrong much more imagina-
tively than Dodo.* Georges thought only of reaching orgasm, fast,
whatever the approach or position and as long as the room
was properly lit. Jeanne dreamed of a scenario, of sets and
costumes.

*I simply wish that, now and then, he would think of using the
cologne I bought at Prisunic on boulevard Gallieni and that he
hasn't even taken out of its box. And that he would clean under
his nails which are so full of earth (am I asking too much?). And
instead of his mad gardener's smock, could he not put on the
jacket I had made for him at Smadja on boulevard Séguin and
which he's only worn to little Mado's funeral. (A cream jacket to
a funeral!) Before he does his thing, I would love him to read me
some of Rimbaud's poetry. He could recite:*

Elle est retrouvée!
Quoi? – L'éternité.
C'est la mer mêlée
Au soleil.*

* from Arthur Rimbaud *Une Saison en Enfer: Délires II*, 'Alchimie du verbe'.
It is recovered.
What? – Eternity.
In the whirling light.
Of the sun on the sea.
– Translation by Paul Schmidt

But I'm dreaming – dreaming! If he does ever open a book, it's a
botanical encyclopaedia. On Sunday he declared in front of our
driver, who prefers the company of gentlemen, and Dodo knows
that perfectly well, that poetry is 'the realm of deviants'. Poor
Nadir went bright red. Such a discreet boy who spends his time
reading and sings so beautifully! Besides, Dodo knows that I love
music and it calms my nerves . . . but he never thinks of winding
up the gramophone before doing what he does at these times,
rather badly and a deal too fast.

A hairy, long-legged shiver skitters over Mirabelle's belly. She
has just pictured her mother, through the mosquito net in
their bedroom in Oran, and her father, in his smock, covered
in soil, brusque and clumsy between the open thighs. The
euphoric, painful distortion of Georges's face, Jeanne's impatient sigh. A ring on the doorbell makes Mirabelle jump.

Héloïse is dressed in stationer's paperclips linked together by
gold thread. At her neck is an amethyst that, on the day of
the great sharing out, had been eclipsed by the stuffed panther.
Her mascara has run and given her a black eye.
    'Were you crying, my darling?'
    'Haven't you seen the papers?'
    'I've done the crossword.'
    'They passed the law.'
    'Oh, yes . . . well . . . I heard that on the radio . . . But it
was a forgone conclusion . . . The polls have been saying so
for months . . .'
    'I'll leave the country.'
    'You're talking nonsense! Where would you go?'

'To the States with Lawrence and the twins. They'll go to the lycée in New York. Will you come with us?'

'To that country of crazies? Their social security pays a life stipend to citizens with health insurance who commit never to eat in fast food places! Héloïse . . . it's the world turned upside down . . . They had the death penalty until 2021! Not to mention that the referendum might well have been rigged, because I read an article—'

'They can't be rigged, *maman*! Ask anyone you like! You don't need to look any further! Ask that twit Marine how she voted! Ask Barnabé!'

'Barnabé?'

'He told me his daughter could be raped or killed at any moment . . .'

'Always the same arguments.'

'Lethal injection! Why not the guillotine out on place de la République?'

'Don't cry over it . . . It looks as though it will be very little used, in practice. Someone from the government was explaining on the radio. My darling . . . such are the twists and turns of history . . . And France is fundamentally well-meaning, I feel.'

'They used to call this "the land of human rights" . . .'

'Your grandmother Jeanne would have been sad . . . She wept with joy in '81! And she wasn't the sentimental kind . . . She was thinking of the war, you see . . . She hugged us both, Violette and me . . . There was a big street party in Pas-de-la-Mule. You were four. You sat on Lawrence's knees of course . . . you clung to him like a baby koala. When we got to the dessert, *maman* told us about an erotic dream she'd had: Robert

Badinter was making love to her at the foot of the guillotine . . .
Your dress is fabulous! Did you make it yourself?'

'It's by a big fashion designer . . . Someone lent it to me.'

'What a life you lead!'

'*Maman* . . . '

'You do! I would have loved to live like you do . . . People
lending me dresses . . . Paying me to be happy . . .'

Bald. The title of the exhibition blinks against the white wall,
inside a garland of lit bulbs, like those signs for variety shows.
The tungsten filaments give out the colour of the twentieth
century. The text of the law banning the sale of incandescent
light bulbs within the European Union is reproduced on the
right-hand side of the wall. Héloïse used to love those old
bulbs. She has kept whole multipacks of them. She bought
up the last stocks of the last shops where they were sold. She
has never got used to the fluorescent bulbs that flatten colours
like an August sky flattens the zinc and limestone of Paris,
runs a crude milky wash over the delicate pink of pale skins.

Hunched and slow, Mirabelle advances holding on to Héloïse's
arm. A buffet runs along one wall of the great chatter-filled
hall. Two maîtres d' are defending the petits fours from a pre-
emptive assault. They have instructions. A black ribbon bars
entry to the exhibition, as if the crowd of guests might amass
behind the starting line and face off in a timed race through
the photos. Héloïse's hand shakes firm, bony and sweaty
hands. Cheeks brush cheeks. She is complimented on the
paperclip dress and her court shoes, which are covered in
chickpeas. Héloïse lays one hand on the rounded tummy of

Pilar, who lets her head rest on Krishna's shoulder. 'Your daughter will be born into a world of sanctioned murder.' At the back of the room, before a photograph entitled *France, It's a Small World*, Barnabé interrupts the journalist from *La Nouvelle Aurore*. The expression 'lethal injection', which no one has pronounced more than four or five times since they were born, trips off every tongue. The word 'lethal'. The hollow feeling in the stomach as the word is said. Barnabé fumes. He jostles the guests aside, makes it to the still-intact buffet and reaches towards a meanly filled flute of champagne, when a gloved hand catches his wrist. Barnabé calls the maître d' an immature citizen, a kamikaze socialist, a defender of rapists and genocides, an enemy of France. The maître d' – a young Indian, hardly twenty years old – allows him to empty the glass in one gulp and swipe a murderous swathe out of the platter of tapenade and asparagus petit fours. Barnabé voted with his soul and his conscience. He voted with 58 per cent of the French people. He told Héloïse: 'I'd understand that my punishment would be death should I violate another person's life.' And Héloïse: 'It's me; I'm your capital punishment, you little fool.' And Lawrence's voice among the daffodils in the Tuileries, unable to stop trumpeting that the last time he fucked Violette was in January of that long ago year, 1977, and that it was most probably Ange, the gardener at Sciroccu, who had fathered Barnabé, considering all those wild embraces at siesta hour in the month of March, as witnessed by the titillated picks and rakes in the toolshed. Barnabé empties another glass of champagne while his memory revives with photographic precision the gardener's tanned features and Habsburg jaw, which he has inherited. He guesses why

Violette made up both a naval officer father and a paediatrician father for him. A cloud of smoke makes him cough, dryly. He spits an asparagus tip out onto the hand of someone next to him: Rosa Winkel, a cigarette wedged in the dark fold of her lipsticked mouth, who wipes her hand and takes three big drags, then rapidly expels them through her nostrils. The maître d', the other one, whose moustache ends in great gelled curlicues, hastens around the buffet to explain to Rosa that it is not permitted to smoke inside the gallery, calling her *Monsieur* at the start of his sentence and *Madame* at the end. He says that the smoke might damage the artworks, whereupon he raises both hands to his own neck, suggesting that they genuinely risk suffocating a photograph. In reply, Rosa merely points to her bustier on which the words 'MY GRANDDAD BUILT AN OVEN FOR JEWS' are scrawled in stem stitch. Lacking a retort, the moustache returns to his place behind the buffet. Héloïse overhears this exchange just as a journalist from the *Herald Tribune* asks her about the meaning of *France, It's a Small World* – a portrait of a red-headed corpse photographed on the sliding stretcher of a freezer drawer in a morgue. Héloïse says she's an unknown woman, that there is no meaning, that she knows nothing about it, that she will die as ignorant as a baby, as uncertain as a raindrop on a bayleaf and just as naughty as a fourteen-year-old whose hand forages under the elastic of a tight, rustling pair of underpants. Héloïse wonders when Rosa started dying her hair blonde. Her muse makes a pathetic sight. The foundation, the ruined face. The over-large dress, empty, gone to seed. And in the transparency of her blue eyes, the light of pride and of hopeless disappointment. Rosa had been beautiful. Her body had worked in every kind of landscape. Very soon, she had acquired the restless expression of youth whose end is in sight. The anguish of heroes whose days are counted. One morning, beneath the fresco of cherubim that formed the background to *Drowned Women,* Héloïse had sat on the naked Rosa. They were celebrating their triumph over the brevity of everything. Héloïse knew the magical power of her beauty, her narcissus-like enchantment and its consoling virtues. Knowing herself, at every moment, beautiful and sought-after. Loving herself in all the reflections in her life – mirrors, shop windows, knife blades, the aroused stares of men she met – to the point of being invaded by pleasure, a stranger to herself. Day after day guessing at the miracle of her face in the world, sustaining her own lustre like a sexual thirst, like the punch of pride when one receives a trophy or a dizzying, undeserved compliment. The ordinary injustice of beauty. Its haphazard lightning bolt. Héloïse hovers in the memory of that morning when the cherubim were shocked to see her crouching over Rosa, clad in pleasure. The *Herald Tribune* journalist makes her excuses and her cheeks flush – the microscopic digital Dictaphone she was holding up to Héloïse's mouth hasn't recorded. They'll have to go back to the beginning.

'All the better because it wasn't a stranger in the morgue, it was a woman who used to spend every day at the Robert-Koch Paediatric Hospital . . . a demented tramp in a wedding dress that was worn to rags. I saw her in the waiting room in A & E when I was very little . . . I'd cut open my head . . . needed four stitches . . . She was yelling over and over, like a stuck record: "Those sons of bitches laughed their heads off seeing

me without a stitch out there on the street!" The nurses used
to give her medicine and blankets. The guys in A & E . . . the
cleaners . . . everyone knew her. She died between two bins
in the car park. She'd been engaged to a German soldier during
the war – Hans-Jakob – who had promised to come back and
marry her when the war was over, and to take her to his village
in Bavaria. She never heard from him again. They shaved her
head on VE Day. And can you see . . . there . . . the man next
to the fire extinguisher . . . beneath the photo *Barnabé's Lice*?
He came to Paris in 1945. He was eight and he saw that woman
as he was getting out of the train . . . that very woman. Her
name was France Sauveur. He saw her breasts. I married him
last month . . . I've taken his name . . . *Calvagh*. It means bald
in Gaelic.'

XXI

Inside the Statue of Liberty's crown.

'I don't see what's bizarre about it.'

'I said *humiliating*.'

'When you have a headache, do you take an aspirin and feel humiliated?'

'That's not the same at all.'

'Yes it is. It's a chemical product that affects your body.'

'Héloïse, I'm an old man. I'm a thousand years old!'

'You've just climbed 354 steps!'

'You practically carried me!'

'I helped you with the last five steps! I was more out of breath than you! I'm also a thousand years old.'

'What sunlight, my lion . . . Look how beautiful it is . . .'

'So it's over? You won't fuck me any more? I'll have to masturbate looking at the Brooklyn Bridge through the window?'

'Scarlett . . . let's not argue . . . I don't want any magic pills. And to get it up, certainly, I've only to look at you . . . What have you done to yourself?'

'Nothing. It was the dog.'

'The dog again!'

'He trembles every time I go near him. He must have been beaten by his previous owners.'

'Is it deep? Is it infected?'

'Just a scratch.'

'One day, you'll bring him his bowl and he'll eat you up instead of his food. He's been in street fights! You picked the most crazed of them all! This time you have to take him back – straight back to the kennels! You understand?'

'He arouses me.'

'The dog arouses you?'

'I want him to attack me . . .'

'And what do you mean by that, Mademoiselle Herschel?'

'We could take off his leash . . .'

'My little obsessive . . .'

'I would undress . . . Lie down completely naked in the courtyard of our building, near the kennel . . . He barks . . . He approaches me . . . The drool drips from his muzzle onto my belly . . . I see his canines . . . the great black and pink gums . . . I smell his breath . . . He bites at nothing . . . GNASH! GNASH! GNASH! and at each gnashing of his jaws I get more afraid . . . You kneel down between my legs . . . you lick my pussy . . . The dog puts his paw on my breast . . . He barks at my mouth . . . I'm so afraid I wet myself . . . I weep in panic . . . You push your tongue into my vagina . . . You make me come . . . The dog catches my thigh in his mouth . . . teeth deep into the muscle . . . You beat his back . . . He lets me go . . . My heart is exploding with fright and pleasure . . . The dog has mad yellow eyes . . . a strange yellow . . . He has an erection . . . You go away. You leave me alone with the dog.'

Translator's Acknowledgements

It has been enlightening and a privilege to work directly with
Émilie de Turckheim on this translation. Heartfelt thanks are
due to my hardworking readers and cultural resources Harold
Lewis, Pauline Le Goff, Clémence Sebag and Ana Fletcher. A
special thank you, too, to my husband Peter Stanton, who
knows more about trimming pipes in reduced circumstances
than I do.

Sophie Lewis
Rio de Janeiro 2014